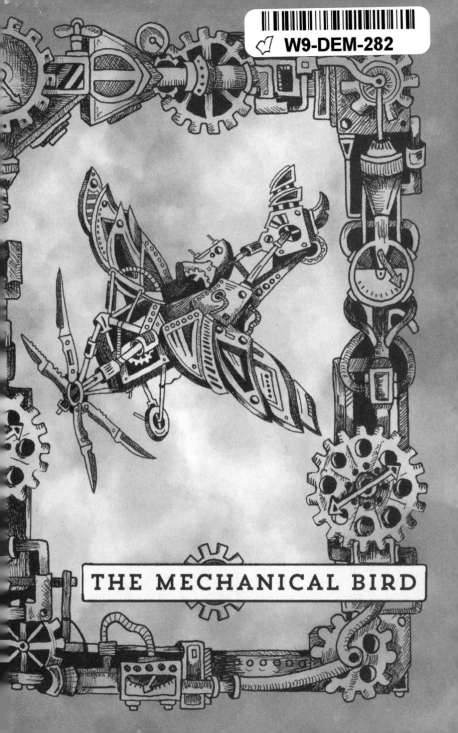

THE MECHANICAL BIRD

ESCAPE TO THE ABOVE

★"A heartfelt tale filled with whimsy, wonder, and magic . . .
truly satisfying."

—*Publishers Weekly*, **starred review**

"**Funny, compassionate, and entertaining** . . . Readers will be immersed
into this dark yet humorous world filled with unique characters."

—*School Library Journal*

"**A fast-paced, refreshingly creative adventure** that will
thrill readers from the very first page."

—Shannon Messenger, *New York Times*–bestselling author of the
Keeper of the Lost Cities series and the Sky Fall series

"**Fabulous characters and a unique mythology** combine to create
something really wonderful. *Snared* **will ensnare you.**"

—Michael Scott, *New York Times*–bestselling author of
The Secrets of the Immortal Nicholas Flamel series

"*Snared* is **pure dungeon-crawling fun**. Witty and page-turning,
I never knew what cheerful mayhem was waiting just around the
bend. **I can't recommend it enough.**"

—Zack Loran Clark, coauthor of *The Adventurers Guild*

"**An imaginative blast of dungeon-crawling adventure** with hilarious
monsters and dastardly traps. **Zany, heartfelt fun for everyone.**"

—Lou Anders, author of the Thrones and Bones series

"*Snared* is chock-full of **quirky characters, fantastic world building,
and wild, hilarious adventure** with every turn of the page.
I loved it, and kids will love it too!"

—Liesl Shurtliff, *New York Times*–bestselling author of *Rump*

"**A thrilling fantasy adventure full of humor and heart.** Adam Jay
Epstein has created a fun, magical world readers will want to stay lost in."

—Jeff Garvin, author of *Symptoms of Being Human*

SNARED
ESCAPE TO THE ABOVE

ADAM JAY EPSTEIN

{Imprint}
MAKE YOUR MARK

New York

SQUARE
FISH

An imprint of Macmillan Publishing Group, LLC
175 Fifth Avenue, New York, NY 10010
mackids.com

Our books may be purchased in bulk for promotional, educational,
or business use. Please contact your local bookseller or the Macmillan
Corporate and Premium Sales Department at (800) 221-7945 ext. 5442 or
by email at MacmillanSpecialMarkets@macmillan.com.

Library of Congress Control Number: 2017958061

ISBN 978-1-250-30871-9 (paperback) | ISBN 978-1-250-14689-2 (ebook)

[Imprint]
MAKE YOUR MARK

@ImprintReads
Originally published in the United States by Imprint
First Square Fish edition, 2019
Book designed by Eileen Savage
Square Fish logo designed by Filomena Tuosto
Imprint logo designed by Amanda Spielman

1   3   5   7   9   10   8   6   4   2

AR: 6.0 / LEXILE: 820L

mackids.com

*A trap's been set for all who steal; your flesh shall be
a maggot's meal, poison darts will strike your shoulder,
before you're crushed by giant boulder.**

**If, on the other hand, you plucked this book off the shelf
hoping it would reveal a secret passage, simply return it to its
proper place and no harm will befall you.*

FOR OLIVE AND PENNY

TABLE OF CONTENTS

1

THE TRAPSMITH OF CARRION TOMB

Giant-slug slime is a sticky mess to clean up. It isn't like troll sweat, which forms yellow trickles along the cracks in the ground and can be easily soaked up with a rag. Or better yet, like dragon drool, which evaporates as soon as it makes contact with the ground. No, giant-slug slime hardens quickly into a thick sap that holds fast to every surface it touches.

With a sigh, Wily pulled out his pocket chisel and began to scrape the green-speckled gunk off the stone floor of the summoning chamber. Cleaning up was the most boring of all his trapsmith duties, but it was also really important. If Wily didn't remove the fallen shields and weapons of the countless knights, wizards, and elves who were captured in the attempt to loot the legendary hidden treasures of Carrion Tomb, they'd be piled up all the way to the ceiling by now.

As trapsmith, Wily was responsible for keeping the underground tomb operating smoothly. First and foremost, he designed, built, and fixed all the traps that were hidden throughout the snaking corridors and gloomy chambers. But that was just the tip of the stalagmite. He also had to feed and train the magical beasts, sharpen the swords of the hobgoblets, and degrease the doors to make sure they squeaked spookily. He was in charge of decorating the tomb as well, carefully placing skulls and rusty shackles to set the spine-chilling mood. In spite of all these important duties, though, he seemed to spend most of his time cleaning.

"Many apologies for the mess," burbled a giant slug in Gargletongue from a shadowy corner of the chamber. "When I'm nervous, I tend to slime a lot."

The slug, which was three times as tall as Wily and had green and red stripes that stretched from her head to her tail, peeked out from behind a stone column.

"It's nothing to feel bad about," Wily gargled back. "You did a great job knocking out this gwarf. He was a sneaky one. Got past a lot of the traps. But not you."

Wily gestured to the short and stocky gwarven warrior passed out in his equipment wagon, snoring heavily through his potato-size nose and braided nostril hair. The giant slug lifted her eyestalks proudly.

"I grabbed him with my tail and shook him just like you taught me," the slug replied modestly.

Once the last glob of slug slime was finally dislodged, Wily grabbed a brush and dustpan off the side of his equipment wagon and swept the bits into a bucket he had made from the steel boot of a captured knight. Then he stepped back to survey his work; the ground glimmered ominously in the flickering light of the wall-mounted torches. Wily thought that Stalag, the master of Carrion Tomb and his surrogate father, would be pleased.

Bending down, Wily picked up a cloth satchel that had fallen off the shoulder of the gwarf during his battle with the slug. He loosened the drawstrings and peered inside to find a large chunk of unsalted meat. Although it smelled terrible, he threw it into a bin mounted on the side of his wagon. It would make a small but tasty treat for the amoebolith. (The trick with all monstrous blobs was to feed them just enough to prevent them from shriveling, while keeping them always hungry and eager to swallow up a trespassing knight.) Fortunately, they weren't picky eaters.

"I'll be more tidy next time," the giant slug gargled as Wily wheeled the equipment cart toward the chamber's exit archway.

Wily pushed the wheeled equipment cart down a wide hall, leaving the summoning chamber and giant slug behind. He was careful to avoid the pressure plates checkering the floor. If he accidentally stepped on just one, it would trigger a spike to drop down from the ceiling, and that would be very bad. Each spike was pointy enough to pierce through an iron helmet as if it were warm candle wax, leaving one with a rather nasty scrape. Wily knew because he regularly sharpened the spikes himself.

Twenty-three steps forward. Seven to the right. Another eighteen ahead. And finally five to the left.

For most people, making it down the hall without triggering a hailstorm of spikes was impossible. Yet for Wily it was second nature. He had been back and forth through this hallway thousands of times.

Wily Snare had lived inside Carrion Tomb for as long as he could remember. He wasn't exactly sure how long that had been, because without ever seeing sunlight (or moonlight for that matter), it was very difficult to keep track of time. For all he knew, he could be ten years old or seventeen or a hundred. Though he was quite sure he wasn't past one hundred, because that's when hobgoblets lost their baby ears and started sprouting their grown-up ones, and that hadn't happened to him yet. Then again, maybe he was a hundred, because not having grown his adult ears yet wouldn't be the only thing that made him different from his hobgoblet brothers and sisters.

Much to his disappointment, Wily just didn't look a lot like the rest of them. His front teeth were all funny, straight and barely poking out of his mouth. His posture was terrible as well: he stood upright and rigid like an arrow, lacking the graceful hunch that his warty-skinned companions possessed. Most embarrassing was the thick clump of long brown hair that sprouted from his head.

Yet the differences weren't all bad; some of them made him uniquely qualified to be the tomb's trapsmith. His long clawless fingers were nimble enough to unscrew the head of the tiniest dart. His small size allowed him to maneuver his way through the gears of the crushing walls when they were in need of greasing. Most important, he wasn't easily frustrated or angered. When he encountered a difficult puzzle, he would simply try a bit harder until he figured it out, instead of smashing things with a spiked club while shouting curse words.

Wily continued pushing his equipment wagon down the hall toward the arched entrance to the library. As he passed through, he got tangled in a veil of silk webbing that had been barely visible in the near-darkness that permeated the entire tomb. Aggravated, he pulled the sticky strands from his cheeks and eyelashes and looked around.

The wooden bookcases lining the library walls were empty; the leather-bound tomes that had once filled them were scattered across the floor. Wily had long ago given up reshelving the books. Each time a new group of invaders made it this deep into the tomb, they'd pull out every single one and toss it on the floor, looking for the clue that would reveal the secret passage to the next hall.

Wily wheeled the equipment wagon to the center of the library, crunching over tattered scraps of parchment on which words had once been written. Before his days, spider saliva had caused the ink to run, leaving dark smudges all over the floor and the pages blank.

"Get out here!" Wily called to the dark recesses of the room.

Seven giant ghost spiders, each as large as a dining table, crawled out from the shadows and across a maze of webs overhead. They weren't actually ghosts, they just looked like them: their exoskeletons glowed with the same pale green color as the spirits of the dead.

"How many times have I told you?" Wily clicked in Arachnid, one of the four languages a trapsmith had to learn along with Grunt, Abovespeak, and Gargletongue. "Webs can be on the walls and the ceiling and covering the secret exits but *not* across the entrance to the library. We don't want to give invaders an early warning. Surprise is everything."

The smallest of the spiders scurried toward Wily, its pointy legs plucking the silk strands of webbing like an out-of-tune harp.

"You never told *me*," hissed the young ghost spider through his mandibles. "I just hatched yesterday."

"Well, where's your mother?" Wily asked, trying to stay calm.

"I ate her this morning," the spider said sinisterly.

"Let's make a new rule," Wily clicked back. "Before you do that, make sure you have her tell you all the rules."

Reaching into his trapsmith belt, Wily retrieved a dozen squirming turtle maggots. He tossed them up into a web that stretched between a bookshelf and the rusted chandelier. The ghost spiders skittered quickly down, racing to be the first to reach the crunchy treats.

Wily didn't stick around to see them fight it out. Spiders really were terrible at sharing. He moved on to the far wall of the library where a dusty tapestry hung and brushed it aside, moving his fingers to a slight indentation in the stone wall. He pressed firmly until he heard the low rumble of rock sliding against stone. The secret exit opened just a few arm's lengths away.

Leaving the ghost spiders to their savage bickering, Wily pushed the equipment wagon out of the library and into a narrow hallway—this was one of Carrion Tomb's many maintenance passages. All the machinery that operated the dungeon's traps was hidden inside these passages, which meant that Wily spent a lot of time in them. This was where he would go to oil the swirling blades of the chop-o-lot, reload the poison darts in the blowgun tunnel, clean the rat cages, stir the sleeping mists, and stoke the flames of the fire-flingers. These passages were also used by the tomb's hobgoblet ambushers and the amphibious fish-headed oglodyte guards to reach their sleeping quarters without having to walk through some of the dungeon's nastier traps, like the scorpion nesting grounds or the crypt filled with bone soldiers.

As he wheeled his wagon down the maintenance hallway, Wily peeked into the neighboring dungeon rooms to check that everything was operating smoothly. He also stopped to peer through a crack in the wall into the Den of Misery and saw that the crab dragon was sleeping soundly; both of its scaly heads snored loudly as it used its gigantic yellow claws as firm pillows. Lately, Wily had been attempting to train the crab dragon to perform simple tricks, but he wasn't having a lot of success; crab dragons were the most dim-witted of all magical crustaceans and also the most temperamental. Wily knew he needed to find another hobby, but there weren't a lot of options in the dungeon; the majority of its hideous inhabitants were single-mindedly concerned with destroying things. Maybe he would try his hand at learning the dragon claw flute.

Reaching a fork in the passage, Wily turned off the main hallway and entered the prison section of Carrion Tomb. His first stop would be the mine entrance, where he would hand over the captured gwarf to the work warden. But he needed to strip the new prisoner down before he handed him over. He unfastened the buckles that held the leather armor in place and tugged off the shoulder plates, exposing a pair of hairy arms and even hairier armpits. He had to turn away from the stink when he removed the boots from the gwarf's four-toed feet. They filled the air with an odor stronger than boiled tunnel trout. He hurriedly peeled off the chest plate and backed away, his hand over his nose.

A journal bound in rat-skin fell to the ground. Wily looked around to see if anybody had noticed, but there wasn't a hobgoblet or oglodyte in sight. He quickly snatched it up, unknotted its thick leather tie string and used his thumb to flip through the pages. To his delight, most of them were filled with maps and words. With a secretive glance, he slid the gwarf's journal into his trapsmith belt, then proceeded into the mine entrance.

"What do you have for me this time?" asked Gu-Har, the wrinkled hobgoblet prison keeper whose dogteeth reached down to his chin.

"A brown-bearded gwarf with plenty of muscle," Wily said as he stealthily shoved the journal deeper into his belt's dangling pouch.

Gu-Har gave the gwarf's arm a jab with his meaty thumb.

"A digger," he said, hoisting the body up over his shoulder.

All the invaders captured in Carrion Tomb were sent to the mines below to live a useful and productive life. Everyone had a purpose. Captured gwarfs were well suited for digging for gold with pickaxes and shovels. Elf prisoners had a great talent for polishing rubies and silver ingots. Squatlings, with their small, round bodies and foldable fairy wings, were ideal for snagging silver nuggets in hard-to-reach places. Humans were perfect to do all the simple jobs that would be too dull for the others, like carrying bags of dirt to the bottomless pit.

The work warden disappeared down the sloping corridor that led to the mine with the gwarf slung over his shoulder, leaving Wily alone again. Like everyone who entered Carrion Tomb, the gwarf had been after one thing: treasure. Just beyond Stalag's study on the lowest level of the dungeon was a vault cluttered with gold, emeralds, talking swords, and hovering crystal orbs. In fact, the vault was so stuffed that it was nearly impossible to enter. The cavern mage, who never threw anything away, had amassed quite a fortune during his questing youth. That had been many, many years ago, though; now, Stalag spent his hours at a stone table in his study, poring over magical texts with the hope of deciphering the secret spells of the ancient subterranean gods.

Wily grabbed the handles of the now nearly empty

equipment wagon and wheeled it down the hall to the salvage room, which was packed tightly with bent swords, dented shields, grappling hooks, and extinguished torches, all of which had been collected from invaders who had foolishly entered the dungeon. Nobody in Carrion Tomb ever ventured to the Above for supplies, which made recycling a necessity. Metal swords were melted down and turned into snap traps for the drop pits. The ropes from grappling hooks were used to repair the constantly fraying dangling bridge over the lava lake. And torches were used as . . . torches.

Wily left the wagon in the middle of the salvage room. He would sort through the gwarf's belongings later; first, he needed to take a closer look at the journal. The truth was, Wily was bored of the tomb. Despite it being all he had ever known, Wily felt as if he were wearing a pair of sandals three sizes too small. He had the strongest feeling that there was something more for him just waiting to be found, a life that would slip on comfortably and never leave him with blisters. In fact, the only time Wily was happy was when he designed a new trap, or when he caught a tiny flicker of life outside the tomb—like he just might with the gwarf's journal.

He moved down a long hallway of heavy wooden

doors, each one fitted with a double dead bolt. These were the sleeping chambers. Nine strides down on the left was one with the picture of a hammer carved above the handle. This was Wily's chamber, his small pocket of privacy in the bustle of the tomb. He cautiously pushed the door open, peered inside, and sniffed to make sure there wasn't anything waiting to jump on top of him.

Satisfied that he was alone, Wily shut the door behind him and double-locked it. He sat down on the furry gray rug he had woven out of slynx fur and emptied the pockets of his trapsmith belt, letting screwdrivers, spare gears, and a tube of lizard mucus tumble out. Pushing aside nails and a vial of unhardened slug slime, he eagerly scooped up the journal and opened it to the first page. He stared at the symbols and letters that danced across the page like fluttering bats.

It was beautiful.

He wished he knew what it said.

The thing was, Wily didn't know how to read. He had a mentor who taught him about gears and levers and mechanisms too complicated to have names of their own, but Stalag had made reading off-limits to all but himself. No one in Carrion Tomb was permitted to even page through a book, let alone read one. Wily had once been daring enough to ask the wrathful mage to make an exception. But Stalag had just screamed at him. *You have enough to learn without words clouding your mind! Back to the traps!* Wily never asked again.

Even so, Wily loved books. He thought about them all the time, even when his attention should have been on his trapsmith duties. During the long, tedious hours cleaning the tomb, Wily imagined all the fascinating things books would tell him if he could only understand their cryptic scribbles. Perhaps it'd be tales, like the ones Stalag used as bedtime stories when he was younger, of the Above and the noble Infernal King who fought the creatures that lurked in the brightness with his mechanical gearfolk. Or maybe the books would describe a distant dungeon that was never invaded and had no need for traps or monsters. He hoped his books would hold tales of adventures with happy endings and stories of families reuniting after many years apart, but he was afraid he would never know. Nobody inside Carrion Tomb could ever tell him what they said.

Wily took his time examining every page of the gwarf's journal, following the curves of the ink symbols with his fingertip. He studied the maps closely, imagining the distant places they depicted. Halfway through, he found a very detailed sketch of a gigantic hand reaching up from the earth, with dozens of pointy fingers sprouting more pointy fingers. He wondered what the rest of this horrifying and fascinating creature looked like. After eyeing every page twice, Wily closed the book.

Rather than unstitch his mattress and slip the gwarf's journal next to the other dozen books he had swiped over the years from captured invaders of Carrion Tomb, Wily put the book back into the pouch of his trapsmith belt. He could steal looks at it later while he was mopping the crypt.

Wily walked over to his worktable and looked down at the model of the Fountain Room he had built. With his finger, Wily moved a small clay figure of a knight through the room. Halfway across, the figure pushed a button on the floor of the model. Two halves of a metal cage popped out of the walls on either side of the knight and came speeding to the center of the room. A cage formed, trapping the figure. Then a trapdoor opened beneath the cage, plunging it, along with the figure, into a pit full of sleeping gas. It was a beautiful trap. Wily had nicknamed it the Wake-No-More. He had just presented it to Stalag, but the cavern mage had brushed it off as being too slow to work. Wily had explained that he could get the two halves to slam shut a bit faster if he put wheels on the bottoms to help them slide. Stalag had told him to go back to the drawing board.

Wily lay down on his cot. He stared at the ceiling of his sleeping quarters and for the thousandth time wondered what might be lurking beyond the mouth of the tomb, in the Above. He desperately wanted to see for himself and, as a child, had often begged Stalag to let him peek. But, of course, that was impossible: Stalag warned him of the sun's power and how its bright rays would melt his hobgoblet skin right off his bones. Stalag had proof of it, too, in the form of a large burn mark on Wily's own arm from his right wrist all the way up to his elbow. When Wily was a toddler, Stalag explained, he had accidentally wandered out of the entrance corridor and into the Above. The sunlight would have left him as nothing more than a skeleton if Stalag hadn't pulled him back inside before it was too late.

And yet, on more than one occasion, only his very keen desire to remain alive had kept him from creeping out for a peek. Wily could never erase the dim hope that somehow something would change, and he would be able to leave the tomb to travel through the mysterious Above.

Wily sighed. He was trapped here in Carrion Tomb like a knight in the Wake-No-More. Even with all his talents, his life was the one trap he couldn't escape from.

He closed his eyes.

It took only a dozen breaths before he was fast asleep.

INVADERS

Dangling by his ankles, Wily hung inside the open trapdoor, his forehead nearly scraping the jagged edges of the rusty snap traps lining the bottom of the pit. He was using a greasy rag to oil the springs of one of them.

"Ninety-seven, ninety-eight," Wily counted with each twist of the rag. "Ninety-nine, one hundred."

Wily stopped his oiling and used his pinky to gently touch the trigger of the snap trap. He pulled his hand away with lightning speed before the jagged mouth of the device smashed closed. Had he been only a fraction of a second slower, his arm would have been pinned inside. Satisfied, Wily moved on to the next rusty spring and started greasing it with the dirty rag.

"One, two, three," Wily started to count again as he continued his tedious chore. "Four, five—"

Suddenly, the black rock attached to the wall just above the shield rack let out a bloodcurdling scream that could wake the dead, which is exactly what it was supposed to do: the bone soldiers in the crypt were harder to stir than an oglodyte after drinking ten mugs of fungus beer.

Wily knew all too well what the sound meant: the tomb was being invaded. Again. Nearly every week, a group of warriors or burglemeisters or acrobats would come marching or tiptoeing or doing double backflips down the entrance corridor of the dungeon. As soon as they passed under the Archway of Many Eyes, the shrieking stones that had been installed all over the tomb would raise the alarm.

This was a pleasant interruption to the boredom of his day. Wily hoisted himself out of the trapdoor and onto the floor of the Chamber of Shield and Helm. He closed the trapdoor with the pull of a hidden lever, untied the rope around his ankles, and hustled over to the maintenance tunnel.

The hallway was still quiet, but Wily knew that in a few moments it would be bustling with cursing hobgoblets, gristle hounds on leashes, and oglodytes coating their tridents with toxic nettle venom.

Wily hurried as fast as his feet would carry him. It would be no problem to get to the tomb's first room, the Temple of Foreboding, before the invaders reached it, but if he was swift enough, he could make it all the way to the maintenance tunnels alongside the entrance corridor. And there, he would be able to eavesdrop on the invaders' discussions before the first trap struck. It was a glimpse of a world he would never know. These conversations were always more interesting than the ones that came after, which were mostly just people yelling things like "Watch out!" and "We need to turn back before it's too late."

To make extra time, Wily took a shortcut around the lip of the Bottomless Pit. As his feet knocked pebbles into the void, he wondered how today's invaders would fare against his traps, and how close they would get to Stalag's treasure.

Nearly out of breath, Wily made it to the entrance corridor just in time for some eavesdropping. He peered through the eyeholes of a stone statue of a bat to see the invaders approaching. Unlike the last batch of scavenging gwarfs, they looked rather impressive, like they might pose quite a challenge: it was a group of four human knights, two male and two female, each with gleaming white armor and a shield bearing a symbol that resembled a golden octopus with no eyes. They strode forward with fearless confidence, their hands resting on the handles of their sheathed swords.

The female commander eyed her shield, which was beginning to sparkle.

"Looks like we may get your wish for a little excitement," she told her companions. "A dragon lies ahead. A crab dragon it would seem by the glow of it."

The four knights pulled out their polished long swords.

"The tongues are mine," demanded the tallest and most broad-shouldered of them.

"And I claim the eyes," the second female knight chimed in, her silver face paint glinting in the torchlight.

"There will be enough crustacean to go around," the commander said.

Wily hoped the crab dragon was well rested. This band of knights looked to be extremely fearsome.

He ran ahead and pressed his eyes up to a hidden slit in the wall of the Temple of Foreboding. He had a clear view as the knights entered the large room.

In the center of the temple, beneath the vaulted cavern roof, the tentacled idol of Glothmurk, goddess of caves and tunnels, stood menacingly. On the far side of the room, a set of crumbling stairs led to a wall painted with a picture of the squid-shaped goddess spewing jets of black slime from the tips of her tentacles down upon a group of chained humans, gwarfs, and elves.

As the knights approached the onyx statue, its mouth opened and spoke with a voice that sounded as if it were coming from the bottom of a deep pool.

"Turn back," it warned the knights, "or be crushed by the might of Glothmurk."

One of statue's black tentacles lifted slowly, pointing back toward the entrance of the dungeon.

"Idol threats do not scare the Knights of the Golden Sun," the female commander said.

She stepped forward, and as she did so, her foot pressed down on a hidden stone pressure plate.

Wily sighed in disappointment. This was going to be over much sooner than expected.

RUMBLE.

All four knights turned to see an enormous stone boulder burst forth from the painting of Glothmurk. It crashed down the crumbling steps and rolled straight into the Knights of the Golden Sun.

The foursome were knocked off their feet and sent flying in every direction. With a metallic clatter, they each hit the ground in a limp pile of armor and limbs.

For the four foolishly brave invaders, their hunt for treasure had reached a quick end.

By taking small steps and using every ounce of his strength, Wily was able to push the stone boulder back up the stairs toward the illusion of a wall. Of his many unpleasant duties, this was his least favorite, even more so than cleaning. No matter how many times he shoved the great rock back up to its resting place, it would always come rolling down again eventually. It felt as if this act was a reflection of his whole life: an endless slog he was doomed to repeat forever.

Wily's arms quivered as he reached the top and pushed the boulder through the fake wall and into the secret room hidden behind it. With a final heave, the great rock rolled into a pair of spring-activated mechanical arms that snapped closed around it.

Wily remembered that this task used to be even worse. When he was smaller, there had been a real wall made of stone that exploded each time the trap was triggered. It was very dramatic, but it took days of backbreaking labor to rebuild, and eventually he had been able to convince Stalag to make do with the current, admittedly less spectacular, setup.

Wily walked down to where the four unconscious knights were lying on the floor. He surveyed the scene. Judging by their size and apparent weight, he knew he wasn't going to get them all down to the prison mine entrance in a single trip. One day soon he would need to build himself a bigger equipment wagon. Wily pulled out a vial of bat venom and placed a single drop on each of the knights' lips. The small dose would keep them sleeping for hours.

"Wily," a scraggly voice said, "do you want a hand with them?"

Roveeka, a lanky hobgoblet with a spine that twisted like a snake up her curved back, approached. Wily had shared a special bond with Roveeka since before he could remember, and there was a lot to love about her: she was a talented knife tosser, and she never bit him even when she was angry or hungry or pleased. She was just about the best sister a hobgoblet could have.

Granted, Wily and Roveeka weren't *technically* brother and sister. But since they had both been orphaned at an early age and didn't have siblings of their own, they had decided a long time ago to treat each other as family.

"As we wheel them down," Roveeka continued with a twitch of her drooping eye, "you can explain to me how a pulley works. Again."

Since Wily was a small child, he had been mentored in the science of engineering by Stalag. The cavern mage had forced Wily to take apart and reassemble every trap in the tomb until he could perform the task with his eyes closed and one hand tied behind his back. Wily's brain absorbed it effortlessly, like a dry sponge soaking up amoebolith slime. Stalag had challenged Wily to come up with never-scapes, traps so complicated and clever that no creature would be able to escape them. Wily had thought up hundreds, most of them so elaborate that they would never fit in the tomb. In fact, it wasn't long before his own crafting skills surpassed his master's. Yet, despite all his ingenuity (or perhaps because of it), Stalag never seemed pleased or impressed.

Roveeka would often ask Wily to teach her basic engineering, but no matter how many times he explained each principle to her, Roveeka seemed to get confused. She had an incredible brain for a lot of other things. She could identify every kind of rock and list off a hundred facts about each one. She could multiply giant numbers in her head in a matter of seconds. But for whatever reason, she was not mechanically inclined.

"Okay," Wily said as the two of them got down on their knees to lift the first knight. "There are two parts of a pulley. The wheel and the rope that wraps around it."

"That part I know," Roveeka said.

"So the pulley changes the direction of your lifting force," Wily continued excitedly. "It allows gravity to help you lift something really heavy. If you place the pulley on the ceiling and attach one end of the rope to something you want to lift—"

"This is already getting complicated." Roveeka sighed.

"I've barely started," Wily said.

Wily was patient with her just like she had been with him when she tried to teach him how to tell the difference between the five types of lava rocks. Despite his best efforts, they had all looked the same to him.

"Maybe if you drew a picture in the dirt so I could see it," Roveeka said. "You could use Mum."

She pulled a polished curved dagger from her waistband. Roveeka had two special daggers that she kept with her at all times. She called them Mum and Pops, since they were the only ones besides Wily who ever took care of her.

Just then, Wily's small, very unhobgoblet ears perked up when he heard the distant thumping of the cook's drum. Mealtime always followed an invasion, no matter how small. The steady beat made Wily's stomach growl fiercely.

"Last one to the dining room has to help wash the dishes," Roveeka said, dropping the knight's head against the ground and hurrying toward the maintenance corridor.

Wily looked back at the knights passed out on the floor. They wouldn't be waking up for hours. He could bring them down to the mines later, after mealtime. Besides, it wouldn't be the worst thing if one got away. (Every once in awhile, Stalag let one of the prisoners go free on purpose just to spread tales about how impossible the traps of Carrion Tomb were. Adventurers liked challenges and the mine always needed more workers.)

Wily dropped the legs of the knight he was holding and sprinted after Roveeka.

THE TOMB'S COMMUNITY dining hall had a pair of long tables in the center and a few smaller ones against the wall by the water troughs. The bigger ones got the platters with the best cuts of jerky and the freshest mushrooms. Wily, however, preferred the smaller tables, where the competition for food was less intense. He had learned long ago that an elbow to the gut was not worth an extra slice of toadstool.

Sitting at a circular table by the kitchen door, Wily and Roveeka each munched on a roasted lizard toe as a pair of web-handed oglodyte twins wrestled over the last sliver of hairy toad. Like fish, oglodytes each had one large eye on either side of their heads and very small brains. Despite Wily knowing them both for his whole life, the only way he could tell the twins apart was by the shape of their arm spikes. Agorop's were jagged like the serrated edge of a saw, while Sceely's were smooth like the tusk of an arrowhog.

"Thish one's mine," Agorop said as he gave a hard tug on the wad of orange hair still dangling from the toad skin.

"No it tisn't," Sceely said angrily as she flashed three rows of her dagger-sharp teeth. "You've already had six."

"How would you know?" Agorop retorted while trying to pry the end-of-the-meal treat from his sister's moist claws. "You can't count."

"I very well can," Sceely sneered. "I been prac-a-tising."

"Let's hear you then."

Agorop tightened his grip on the toad skin.

"One, two, ten, eight, six," Sceely said confidently.

Agorop went silent. Then, after a considerable pause, he said: "Well, maybe you can. But thish piece is still mine."

Suddenly, a hush came over the room. Even the growling gristle hounds in the corner went still.

Wily turned to the door to see that Stalag himself had entered the dining hall. The cavern mage ate meals on only rare occasions. In the corner of the hall, there was a lone table that always had a bowl of broth placed on it, whether Stalag chose to show up or not. When Wily was younger, he snuck a taste of the mage's broth while the cook was preparing it and quickly wished he hadn't. It was a vile acidic liquid. Little wonder that the mage skipped his meals so often.

Lately, the mage barely looked to be one of the living. It was rumored that he used to be a man or an elf but that the magic had twisted him. His eyes hung in their sockets like sacks of spider eggs: pale, engorged, and quivering from the inside. Only a thin layer of gray skin stretched across his bony frame, and when the torchlight shined from the right angle, his fist-size heart could be seen slowly beating inside his rib cage.

Strangely, Stalag didn't head directly to his private

table like he usually did. Instead, he came to a halt in the middle of the room. His cloudy eyes scanned the dining hall, looking for something or someone. Stalag found what he was searching for and started moving again—straight for the table where Wily was sitting. Roveeka, Sceely, and Agorop fearfully stared down into their laps.

The cavern mage stopped a half stride away from the table. Wily could see the veins in his arms throbbing like maggots eating their way through a piece of spoiled meat. Then Stalag opened his cracked gray lips.

"Snare," his voice whispered like a hot wind from the lava chamber, "I found this in my study."

Stalag reached into his pocket and pulled out a wiggling rat by its tail. The oglodyte twins hunched lower until they were practically under the table. Wily stared at the squirming rodent and hoped dearly that it would bite Stalag's finger with its sharp front teeth.

"It must have escaped from the Chamber of Swarms," Wily said without flinching. "The rat cages have cracks in them. They need to be replaced."

"You're the trapsmith," Stalag coughed. "Build new cages."

"I would, Stalag, but—"

"I told you to call me Father," Stalag hissed.

The command made Wily bristle. This withered man-creature was not his father. Stalag had never said a nice thing to him or cared for him in any way. Forcing Wily to call him Father was just another trick to make Wily do his bidding.

"I'll start melting the steel before bed . . . Father," Wily said, the last word stinging his lips.

"You'd better. Because if I find another rat in my study—"

Stalag tossed the rat onto the table and raised his hands above his head. Arrows of crackling darkness shot forth from his ink-tipped fingernails and struck the rat, disintegrating all but its still twitching tail. Wily felt a pang of sadness for the unfortunate creature.

The cavern mage turned and walked slowly to his table. Only after he was seated and slurping his broth did anyone dare speak once more.

"I thought you were a dead hobgoblet for sure," Agorop said with giddy relief.

"I nearly swallowed my tongue," Roveeka said, looking faint.

"He loves you like a son," Sceely said softly through her sea of teeth.

But Wily knew that Stalag did not like him. He *needed* him because a talented trapsmith took years to train. Wily was permitted to live because he was difficult to replace. Not for the first time, Wily thought about his real parents. Most hobgoblets like him had no families. His own mother and father had been killed before he was old enough to remember them. Stalag had told him the sad story with very little sympathy: his mother and father were killed by a band of gold-seeking thieves in the dungeon's library when he had been just a few weeks old.

Although Wily had never met his parents, he thought a great deal about them. Had they been nifty with traps like he was? Had they shared his odd appearance? And had they longed for a different life in a trapless, treasureless dungeon, too? Would they talk to him like Stalag did? Wily hoped not.

"I thought Stalag was going to slaughter me just for sitting next to you," Agorop continued as he grabbed the rat tail and shoved it into his mouth. "Or worse still, send me up there, to the Above."

The very thought made both of the oglodyte twins shudder.

No one in the tomb but Roveeka shared Wily's fascination with the Above. It was well known inside Carrion Tomb that those who angered Stalag were given what they considered to be the most horrible punishment of all: they were sent to the Above and never allowed to return to the safety of the tomb. Stalag had told them many times about the wall-less barren that lay beyond the entrance of Carrion Tomb. Up there, freezing shards of water fell from massive roofs of smoke. Winged creatures with talons and beaks that were neither bat nor moth flocked overhead. Unchained land beasts without masters roamed free, scavenging for food. Colorful fungus blossoms sprayed potent odors into the air, attracting stinging insects. Even the air itself was wild, tossing objects and shaking the doors. An oglodyte would rather stab herself in both her hearts than face the horrors of the Above . . . but Wily couldn't reconcile how a place that made treasures like the gwarf's journal could be so terrible.

Wily chewed the last bit of meat from the lizard toe before tossing it onto the bone pile. He plucked a mushroom cap from his plate and was about to pop it into his mouth when—

SCREEE.

Everyone turned to the kitchen door. The shrieking stone above its wooden frame was screaming at the top of its nonexistent lungs.

Hobgoblets and oglodytes leaped up and pulled their weapons out from under their seats. Roveeka slid Mum and Pops from her waistband. Stalag put down his soup ladle.

Carrion Tomb was being invaded *again*!

There was no time to lose. Wily had to clean up the last batch of invaders before the new ones stumbled onto them. Wily and Roveeka exchanged worried looks. He knew she was thinking the same thing he was—if Stalag realized how careless Wily had been, the cavern mage would surely lose his patience and disintegrate him just like he had done to the unfortunate rat. Wily pushed through the angry throng of dungeon denizens and sprinted out of the dining hall.

3

THE POISON DART AND
WHERE IT DIDN'T STRIKE

By the time Wily reached the top floor of the dungeon, the latest invaders had already entered the Temple of Foreboding. He was too late. There was nothing he could do about the Knights of the Golden Sun, who were still lying on the floor of the temple chamber. Instead, he ran up to the spy hole hidden in one of the temple wall's carved stone columns. Peering through it, he laid eyes on a rather unusual trio.

One of them was a bald human wearing a tarnished bronze suit of armor that encased him from his shoulders down to his feet. At first glance, he appeared to be like many of the other knights who had foolishly trespassed into Carrion Tomb over the years. Yet there was one drastic difference: this knight's right arm was not attached to the rest of his body. Instead, the arm was hovering next to his empty shoulder socket like a wasp protecting its nest.

The second intruder was a female elf about Wily's height wearing no armor at all. Her cloth tunic and leggings were a strange color that Wily had never seen before: a mix of gray and green, but somehow brighter, too. It matched the long locks of hair sticking out from her scalp. She had a pack strapped to her back that appeared too thin and too loose to have anything inside it at all.

The third intruder was the strangest of them all. Twice the size of the tallest oglodyte, it appeared to be made entirely of moist earth. The creature was coated in thick moss as shaggy as fur, and disks of yellow fungus stuck out from its arms and back. A pair of jeweled stones was embedded in its head where eyes should have been, and it was missing a mouth: more moss was covering the lower portion of the giant's face.

It didn't take the three strange companions long to spy the unconscious bodies of the four knights on the temple floor.

"Hug the wall on the east side of the room," the elf said, her voice as clear as two swords clashing.

"Whatever knocked them out must have come down those steps over there."

They had gotten lucky. The fallen knights were a dead (or rather sleeping) giveaway. Wily hoped dearly that he could clean up this mess before Stalag realized what had happened. Although, on the positive side, he was rather pleased that he wouldn't have to roll the boulder back into place twice in a single day. His shoulders were still strained from the first time.

"Look at that," the bald human said with a frown and a shake of his head. "My old comrades—Knights of the Golden Sun. I remember when they used to fight for the freedom of Panthasos instead of selfishly raiding dungeons for treasure."

"You mean like you do, Pryvyd?" the elf asked.

"Yeah," the knight named Pryvyd replied, "I guess they got smart, too."

Wily watched as Pryvyd smirked. But despite the smile on his face, there was a hint of sadness in his amber eyes. It was hard to believe that this man used to be a Knight of the Golden Sun. They always marched into the tomb with heads held high, armor polished to a reflective shine, and wielding their arrogance like a gleaming sword.

"Turn back," the tentacled idol in the middle of the

room warned them, as it had the previous invaders, "or be crushed by the might of Glothmurk."

One of the idol's black tentacles lifted slowly, pointing back to the corridor from which they had just entered.

Every once in awhile, an invader would actually listen to the threat of the statue and walk right back out of Carrion Tomb. These three, however, were not so easily scared.

"The pointing tentacle is a nice touch," the elf said, smiling to herself. "Just in case we forgot which way we had come in from—ten seconds ago."

The giant of moist earth made a series of hand gestures.

"You think everything with tentacles is creepy," the elf replied.

The giant nodded in agreement, keeping his distance from the statue of Glothmurk.

"I guess we'll be leaving you behind when we explore the Lair of the Ink Queen," the bald human stated.

The giant shivered and nodded even more enthusiastically.

Wily's spy hole was along the east wall, and as the invaders passed by, he got a closer look at the trio, noticing details he hadn't been able to see until then.

He saw that the knight called Pryvyd had a tattoo of an arm with a clenched fist drawn on the back of his olive-skinned scalp; Wily guessed that this was somehow related to his own hovering arm. As the moss giant stomped by, Wily could see that it was not only covered with vegetation but with insects as well. Earthworms slithered across its moist dirt skin and pill bugs nibbled away at the overgrown shoots of green growing from its pores. A line of ants stretched from its right foot up to its stomach, where they poured in and out of its belly button.

Wily could have spent hours (or at least another few seconds) studying the giant, but he became distracted by a strong smell. It was a sticky-sweet odor that reminded him of slightly spoiled yams. He turned his head and realized that he had caught a whiff of the elf's skin. She was passing so close to the spy hole that he felt as if his nose might accidentally touch her.

Just then, the elf stopped and raised her nose, also sniffing the air. *Did she smell him, too?* She turned to the slit in the column and looked through, into the darkness, right at Wily. Without thinking, he ducked out of view. He wondered if she had really seen him peering out or if he had only imagined it.

By the time Wily had pulled himself off the floor

of the maintenance hall and peeked back out into the temple, the intruders had moved on.

He caught up with them as they slowly made their way down the hallway to the armory. Wisely, they were taking their time, carefully inspecting the hallway for traps as they proceeded. But they would find none in the hallway: Wily had long ago discovered that alternating rooms with dangerous traps and rooms with nothing at all kept invaders on edge. Paranoia and fear could be weapons as dangerous as a sharp spike.

"For a tomb with such a fearsome reputation," the elf remarked, "there seems to be a serious lack of peril. They might as well serve snacks and lay out the royal carpet for us."

Just you wait, Wily thought. *It isn't a question of if my traps will catch you, but when.*

"Why does everything always have to be a challenge for you?" Pryvyd asked, exasperated. "Enjoy the moment of peace."

"It's a little thing called 'fun,'" the elf replied. "And easy is boring. And boring isn't fun."

The trio was welcomed to the armory with a chattering cackle. Before them, engulfed in green flames, the Skull of Many Riddles hovered ominously.

"More fuel for my flames," the skull said sinisterly as it flew closer to the invaders.

"Let us pass," the bald knight said, sounding annoyed and aggravated in equal measure, and pulled out his sword with the arm that was still attached to his body.

The skull laughed with diabolical glee as the sword burst into scalding emerald flames. Pryvyd dropped it before his gauntlet began to melt. Wily had told the skull more than once to tone down the theatrics, but it wasn't very good at listening to instructions.

"Your weapons won't help you here," the skull screamed maniacally. "A riddle for your life!"

With another laugh, flames blocked every exit from the room.

"One guess is all you'll get," the skull bellowed, "before you feel my wrath."

The skull asked a new riddle each time someone entered the armory. If the wrong answer was given, it would set fire to the entire perimeter of the room. The thick smoke would cause everyone inside to pass out within moments.

"*What moves up and down but never bends,*" the skull sang. "*The more it stabs the more it mends.*"

Wily was quite fond of these puzzles, and, by

necessity, he had gotten quite good at solving them. He usually needed only a few clues before he figured out the answer.

"It has an eye—"

"A needle," the elf answered before the skull had even finished the question.

"—but cannot . . ." The skull stopped in mid-line. It looked as surprised as a skull could look. "What did you say?"

"A needle," the elf repeated.

Wily was aghast. She had cracked the riddle before he had. No one was ever that smart.

The green flames dissolved as the skull sulked back to its resting place on top of an old suit of armor. Pryvyd picked up his sword.

"Well done," Pryvyd said to the elf. "Quick thinking."

"I've had lots of practice solving them," the elf said. "When I was a child, my parents would tell my older sister and me riddles before we went to bed."

The moss giant made a series of gestures with its large earthen hands.

"Moshul's right," Pryvyd added as he moved for the exit. "I'm sure they're looking down on you now and smiling."

Wily was surprised to hear such tender words come

from the lips of the intimidating knight. He had never known that a human could have a soft side.

"I don't think they see much from where they are now," the elf replied tersely.

"The lifted see more than you know," the knight said softly.

Wily had heard other invaders call their dead "*the lifted.*" He found it to be a strange term, considering that in his experience, the dead weren't able to lift anything, least of all themselves.

"That's a magic I don't believe in," she said curtly. "Let's just get what we came for."

As if a torch had been set aglow, Wily looked at the elf in a different light. She had lost her parents, too, and she seemed to really miss them. It was a feeling he understood well.

The three invaders reached a fork in the hallway.

"Which way do you think?" Pryvyd asked, pointing to the left and then the right. "Certain death or unquestionable doom?"

"I'm feeling 'unquestionable doom' for a change," the elf answered.

"Oh," Pryvyd said with a sigh, disappointed. "And I was going to go with 'certain death.' Moshul, do you want to be the tiebreaker?"

Moshul suggested neither. Instead, he favored turning back toward the Skull of Many Riddles.

"You know that's not happening," the elf said.

Moshul pointed in the direction the elf girl had.

"'Unquestionable doom' it is," Pryvyd said as they made their way to the right toward the ale cellar.

It was a poor choice. They would have had a better chance evading capture if they confronted the bone soldiers in the Death Crypts. Wily hurried ahead to find a hidden spot in the cellar with a clear view.

The ale cellar reeked of stale mushrooms and alcohol. Gigantic wooden barrels lined the walls, each big enough to store ten thousand swigs of ale. The door on the other side of the cellar was guarded by the oglodyte twins, Agorop and Sceely. Agorop was dozing on a bench while Sceely kept patrol, marching up and down the cellar as she picked her crooked teeth with a rusty arrow.

The invaders snuck in and took cover between the toadstool juicer and a barrel. From a distance, they silently watched Sceely make her rounds, waiting patiently for the right opportunity to strike.

After three circles of the cellar, when Sceely was about halfway back to her dozing companion, she stopped and bent over. She pulled off her boot and gave it a shake to remove a pebble or two from the inside. As Sceely was busy looking down, the elf whispered something into the bald knight's ear. At once, Pryvyd left his cover and made a speedy and silent approach.

Pryvyd pulled his sword and was about to attack Sceely when the lids of the barrels were sent flying. Dozens of hobgoblet ambushers came flooding out of the empty barrels with clubs and swords in hand.

Sceely turned to Pryvyd with a devilish look in her eye.

"Yoosh been narbungled!" she hissed. (Oglodytes have thirty-two different words for ambush. *Narbungle* is the most insulting of them all. It means "You fool! You should have seen that attack coming, but you didn't and now you'll pay.")

Pryvyd was swarmed with hobgoblets, a surge of bald heads and hunched backs charging at him from every direction. The hobgoblets had a tendency to get over-excited and actually cause harm to the invaders. Wily had told Stalag many times that the hobgoblets needed to be reprimanded, but the mage didn't seem to care.

Wily's view was partially blocked, so he couldn't

see exactly what was happening, but he could hear the sound of clanging and metal scraping against armor. Then, to his surprise, he started seeing hobgoblets fall.

Pryvyd plowed through the crowd of hunched ambushers, using his spiked shield not only to protect himself, but also as a weapon. The shield alone wasn't enough to keep his attackers away, though. A pair of furious hobgoblets charged Pryvyd from behind, knives held high. The knight didn't have a chance to spin around to face his attackers; he was too busy with the ones in front of him.

SMACK. SMACK.

The furious hobgoblets were both knocked unconscious by the flat side of a sword. Wily was baffled. *Who is holding the weapon? Certainly not Pryvyd, who is a few feet away.*

A third hobgoblet was struck in the back of the head by the blunt end of the weapon.

Wily looked closer to see that the sword was being handled by Pryvyd's enchanted floating arm. Pryvyd and his arm were each fighting independently! And they made an incredible team. It was like a synchronized dance of blade and shield.

The sight was so strange, the remaining hobgoblets stopped and lowered their clubs. They tilted their heads as if trying to figure out what was keeping the arm afloat. Their pondering was cut short by Pryvyd, who charged at them with his spiked shield. The hobgoblets scrambled to get out of the way, but, still disoriented, found themselves tripping over one another's stubby feet. The floating arm made fast work of the remaining, stumbling ambushers.

"Well done, Righteous!" Pryvyd called out to his hovering arm.

Meanwhile, on the other side of the ale cellar, a group of knife tossers had begun flinging daggers at Moshul and the elf, who had jumped on its back. Moshul picked up a pair of the large barrel lids and used them as shields to block the incoming daggers. The elf returned fire by plucking violet mushrooms from the giant's backside and hurling them at their attackers. Wherever the mushrooms landed, they exploded in a burst of noxious yellow vapors. The hobgoblets coughed violently before collapsing.

Within moments, thirty hobgoblets lay scattered on the cellar floor, and the oglodyte twins cowered in the corner.

"Let ush live," Sceely pleaded as the victorious invaders approached. "We didn't know they'd be jumping out at you—all killy and the like."

"We thought it was one of them surprise parties," Agorop continued, "and you were the guests of honor."

"Thash right," Sceely agreed. "We did."

"Honest truth." Agorop gave his most cowardly smile.

The twins might not have been very good at counting, but they were even worse at lying.

The elf plucked another mushroom off Moshul's back and tossed it at the oglodytes. The cloud of yellow knocked them unconscious.

Wily was impressed that the invaders had made it through the first three chambers with no injuries. He couldn't recall anyone ever doing that before. Fortunately, he knew the trap awaiting them in the next corridor would be the first real test of their luck and courage.

The Trip Wire Tunnel was one of Wily's masterpieces. Thin, barely visible strands of wire were strung all along the narrow hall. If one was as much as touched by a clumsy foot, a spinning hammer would pop up from the floor and crack a toe (or five).

Of course, any truly careful intruder would be able to spot the wires. But that was where Wily's true brilliance showed itself, because it wasn't the trip wires and the spinning hammers that made this tunnel dangerous. They were merely the distractions from the real trap: halfway down the hall, between a pair of trip wires, there was a set of pressure-sensitive plates in the ground. As soon as they registered even the tiniest weight on them, a poison dart was fired from a blowgun hidden in the wall. So far, nobody had ever seen it coming: the first member of each group of invaders was always struck by the dart. The poison inside was made from the venom of a pale cobra, and its effect was instantaneous: intense swelling followed by a coma that lasted for a hundred hours.

Wily hurried over to the midpoint of the tunnel to check that the dart was filled with poison. From his position, he could see that the trio had stopped before the tunnel's first trip wire.

The giant studied the path. After a moment, he made a series of gestures to the others.

"Your feet aren't that large," Pryvyd said dismissively. "You'll be fine."

The giant repeated the gestures again slower and more clearly.

"Moshul may be right," the elf said. "Who knows what these wires trigger. I'm certain I can make it across without touching one of them, and at least one of us needs to get to the other side of the tunnel to reach the treasure. . . ."

"I suppose that does make sense," Pryvyd said. "I'll follow behind, and Moshul will bring up the rear."

The mountain of moss seemed very pleased with their decision.

Wily watched as the elf stepped up to the first wire. She spun around and did a triple backflip, effortlessly avoiding the first three trip wires. Her strange-colored hair bounced as she cartwheeled over the next two. She was tumbling right into his trap, completely unaware.

"This is even easier than it looks," she called back to the other two.

Wily took measure of the elf's height—she was just a couple fingers shorter than him. He adjusted the angle of the blowgun's nozzle so the dart would strike her directly in the neck as she made her next series of flips.

She would be struck as soon as she bounded over the eighth trip wire. The last sound she would hear before falling into a deep sleep would be a gentle *whit* as the dart sailed through the air.

"Odette, don't let the everstuff satchel slip from your back," Pryvyd called out.

"Keep your eyes on the wires and not on me," the elf called as she tightened the straps of the silk shoulder bag.

Odette.

Wily suddenly felt queasy. The elf had a name. His

head began to swim as if he were standing too close to one of the sulfur vents in the Lair of Living Flame. *Did I eat an undercooked chunk of lizard toe?* The sickly sensation was getting worse by the second. Wily's head was spinning. *It is amazing how quickly Odette solved that riddle. She is really very smart. . . .*

He had to focus on the task at hand. He should be glad. Odette would be an easy cleanup, just a quick heave into the equipment wagon. Then she would spend the rest of her life a prisoner, toiling in the mines. *So what if it seems as if we could be friends? I wonder if she would help me with that new trap I'm working on.*

Odette arched her back over the seventh trip wire. . . .

Wily reached out and smacked the end of the blowgun just as Odette flipped over the eighth wire, unwittingly setting her foot down on the pressure plate. *Whit.* The dart shot out and struck the stone floor by her feet. Startled, she stepped back, knocking into the trip wire.

A spinning hammer rose up from the floor and just missed her heel.

Odette looked down at the poison dart.

"Are you okay?" Pryvyd called out.

"Yes," Odette answered, "but watch where you step."

Odette eyed the wall with the blowgun thoughtfully

before continuing on, carefully stepping over the next trip wire.

Wily wasn't sure what had come over him. He was hit by an avalanche of regret. He had the horrible feeling that by letting Odette pass through the Trip Wire Tunnel, he had made a very foolish mistake, a mistake that would cost him dearly.

4

THE VAULT

By the time Wily snapped back to attention, Odette and her companions had already left the Trip Wire Tunnel and were inside the Fountain Room, which was appropriately named for the large fountain in the shape of a gwarven maiden. Cool, clear water used to pour out from her open lips in a steady stream until recently, when an angry invader had used his axe to remove the head of the statue. Now, the water just dribbled out from her neck and down her body.

The fountain was a trap, of course: whoever drank from it was instantly transformed into a salamander. But since Stalag had placed the fountain there, not one person had actually been stupid enough to taste its water. Everyone simply walked by it and through one of the two doors on the other side of the room. Wily had told Stalag many times that they needed to replace the fountain with one of the devious never-scapes he had designed, like the ankle shocker, which filled the room with knee-deep water and a dozen electric eels. But as usual his suggestion had been ignored.

Moshul came to a stop before the fountain and began tapping his foot against the ground.

"You hear something?" Pryvyd asked as he watched Moshul bend down and put his head against the floor.

"Well, considering the fact that he doesn't sleep," Odette interjected, "I think we can assume he isn't stopping to take a nap."

After a long listen, Moshul lifted his head again. He made a series of hand signals to his companions that ended with him pointing his finger to the floor.

"Directly below?" Odette asked.

Moshul nodded, his jeweled eyes twinkling in the torchlight.

"Sounds like a good shortcut to me," Pryvyd said.

Wily was puzzled. There was no secret door in the floor. *What is the knight talking about?*

"They are doing very well," a voice said quietly from behind Wily.

Wily turned to see Roveeka hunched next to him.

"I'm glad you weren't assigned to the ambush in the ale cellar," Wily said.

"Me too," Roveeka replied. "The dining hall is going to be much less crowded at the next meal. I might even get a full portion for a change."

"You always do see the positive side of things," Wily responded.

BOOM.

Wily's attention was pulled back to the invaders. Moshul was pounding the ground with his mighty fist, causing the entire Fountain Room and the maintenance tunnel to shake.

"Be careful, Moshul," Odette said, stepping back from the spot where the earth giant was striking the ground. "We don't want the whole floor giving way."

Another series of blows shattered the stone, creating a hole in the Fountain Room.

Pryvyd approached and stuck his head into what moments ago had been solid rock. From Wily's perspective, he couldn't tell how deep it went, but it certainly seemed to go down more than an arm's length.

"All clear," Pryvyd said before moving back.

Then the moss giant stepped up to the hole and jumped inside. Legs, body, and head all disappeared. After a second, Wily heard a loud thud.

"Where'd it go?" Roveeka asked, completely dumbfounded.

"I don't know," Wily replied, equally stunned by what he'd just seen.

Next, Odette jumped into the hole, followed by Pryvyd.

They were gone—only the hole was left.

Wily tugged the lever on the wall of the maintenance passage, where he had been observing the intruders, opening a door to the Fountain Room. He hurried over to the hole and looked inside.

The hole went straight down to the cavern with the Underground Lake—he could see faint light reflections dancing on the surface of the water, and then he heard the noises of battle from far below: the three invaders must have caught the Guardian of the Lake, a giant cave squid, by surprise. He leaned farther into the hole to see: the invaders were attacking the Guardian from behind, striking its unprotected head while the creature's tentacles flailed helplessly.

Wily's heart lurched: the invaders had cheated! They

had avoided his most elaborate traps, skipping past the freezing pools, the drop nets, the ghost spiders, the crab dragon, and a dozen other clever contraptions, all carefully designed by Wily to bring the invaders' adventurous ways to an end. The cavern with the Underground Lake was just one chamber away from Stalag's study and the tomb's treasure vault.

He had to get down there quickly. He had to do something to stop the invaders before they reached Stalag. Otherwise there would be a lifetime of misery for him.

Wily thought about jumping through the hole, but the portion of the lake below was only knee-deep. Without a giant to catch him, he'd likely break every bone in his body. Instead, he backtracked past the Trip Wire Tunnel, squeezing through the gears and machinery. There was a service ladder near the ale cellar that would take him down to the maintenance passage next to the Chamber of Swarms. When he arrived at the ladder, he found a wounded hobgoblet slowly descending the rungs.

"Out of the way!" Wily called out.

But the hobgoblet didn't look like he was moving anywhere fast. Wily grabbed the two sides of the ladder and slid down until he reached the head of the injured ambusher. He climbed right over him and slid the rest of the way down.

At the bottom, a large group of oglodytes with tridents was waiting to spring out from the secret door to the Chamber of Swarms.

"Move it," Wily shouted as he tried to shove his way past.

"What's the rush, Snare?" a particularly slimy oglodyte asked.

"I've got to stop the invaders from reaching Stalag's study," he said.

"They'll have to get past us first," another oglodyte said, stabbing the air with his trident.

"They already have!" Wily cried.

The oglodytes exchanged puzzled looks as Wily plowed through them.

By the time he reached the tunnel alongside the Underground Lake, he found the squid lying in a black pool of its own ink. It was either dead or had lost the will to fight. Worse still, the invaders were already moving down the final torch-lit tunnel, the one that led straight into Stalag's study, the last room before the vault. No one had ever made it half this far since Wily had become Carrion Tomb's trapsmith.

Wily's mind raced faster than his feet. *What have I done? Why did I let that poison dart miss its mark?* Stalag would be furious to have to dispatch the invaders himself. Wily tried not to imagine the horrible punishments he would face for his failure to prevent their progress earlier. Would he be submerged feetfirst into the lava pool? Or become target practice for the hobgoblet knife tossers? Or . . . would he be banished to the Above?

Pressing his eyes up to a hole in the study wall, Wily watched as the invaders made their entrance.

Behind a great stone table stacked high with magical tomes, Stalag sat in a chair carved from the giant skull of an ancient beast. By his fingers, a black snap-lizard curled its tail around the base of a flickering candle.

"Are you the master of Carrion Tomb?" Odette called out.

"You were foolish to enter," Stalag said in a menacing whisper. "Either surrender now and spend your life working in my mines—or suffer a far worse fate."

"I don't think I want to spend the rest of my life underground," Odette said boldly. "You look like you could use some sunlight yourself."

Stalag grimaced. His frail hands shot into the air. Just like with the rat, crackling darkness flew out like arrows from a crossbow.

In a blur, the magical bolts soared across the room toward Odette's throat.

Odette flipped backward and landed in a split. The

arrows whizzed right over her head and struck the wall behind her instead. She bounced back to a standing position, perfectly unruffled, and raised her eyebrows as if to say, *Is that all?*

"I see you're quick on your feet," the cavern mage hissed, "but I know spells that your acrobatic tricks will not be able to dodge so easily."

While Stalag spoke, Pryvyd flashed a few fingers to the moss giant; it was almost as if he were talking to him without saying any words.

The moss giant charged toward Stalag.

But the old mage was prepared. He snatched a quill from the tabletop and used it to scribble ancient hieroglyphs in the air. A small tornado formed around the symbols, sweeping them up and churning them like dirty undershirts in the laundry cauldron. The blast of air struck the moss giant—and did nothing at all to him.

"You're going to need to do better than that," Odette said with an impish smile.

Stalag's expression hardened. Wily recognized the change; he'd seen it many times before. Stalag was no longer frustrated, he was *angry.*

"Cave ivy, oglodyte's toes, wart on a he-hag's nose," Stalag chanted as he pointed to the snap-lizard taking

cover behind the wax candle. *"Now my anger grows and grows."*

The fork-tongued reptile started to expand exponentially. It took only moments before it was the size of the stone desk. A second later, it took up a third of the room. The lizard darted out its now gigantic tongue to taste the air. Then it opened its jaws, revealing a row of triangular teeth.

Pryvyd stepped in front of his companions and pulled his sword from its sheath.

"Step aside, Pryvyd," Odette called. "I've got this."

The elf reached out and plucked a purple turnip from Moshul's thigh. Both Pryvyd and Moshul looked alarmed.

"Who's hungry?" Odette taunted, then tossed the turnip at the lizard. The giant reptile's tongue grabbed it out of the air and swallowed it whole.

Odette, Pryvyd, and even Moshul dove for the ground.

Stalag just stood there, confused, his eyes darting from the lizard to the prone figures on the ground.

Then the lizard exploded. Chunks of scale and tail splattered all over the room.

Stalag, with fear in his eyes and bits of lizard on his robe, ran for the treasure vault. If he could get to the door, he could lock himself in. Nothing could open it from the outside. The invaders would have to wait until Stalag chose to leave, if he ever chose to at all. Wily knew that the old cavern mage would rather waste away for centuries alone with his gold than hand over a single coin of his precious treasure.

Pryvyd leaped to his feet, grabbed his hovering arm with his other hand, and tossed it like a spear.

"Fly, Righteous!" Pryvyd called out.

The fingers of the flying hand made contact with Stalag's shoulder and clamped down tight. With a tug, the arm known as Righteous pulled the cavern mage to the ground.

Stalag tried to get to his feet, but before he could, the three invaders were towering over him.

"You win," Stalag said with his voice trembling. "Spare my life and take whatever piece of treasure you want."

Wily had never heard his master admit defeat or sound so frightened. It was wonderful. He had to keep himself from smiling.

"We plan on taking every coin of it," Odette said, tapping the pack on her shoulders. "But that's not all—"

And then she said the words that would change Wily's life forever. "We want your trapsmith, too."

5

GROVBLUNDERED

Wily must have heard Odette incorrectly. These invaders couldn't possibly want *him*. He was just an ugly hobgoblet with a tool belt.

"I—I won't give you the trapsmith," Stalag sputtered.

"You're not in a position to bargain," Pryvyd said, extending his sword.

Stalag's face went pale. He tried to crawl backward, but Moshul grabbed him by the ankle before he could get far.

"How about an oglodyte guard?" Stalag pleaded. "Or a giant slug? Or something more impressive, like a crab dragon?"

"Call for the trapsmith," Pryvyd insisted as he

pushed the tip of his sword against Stalag's bony rib cage, "or your skeleton will be a new decoration for the tomb."

The cavern mage's cloudy eyes shifted desperately back and forth.

"You're making a very foolish mistake," Stalag hissed.

"Just the trapsmith," Odette demanded.

As he stared down at Pryvyd's sword, Stalag took a moment to weigh his options. Then he cleared his throat with a strained cough.

"Snare," Stalag called out. "I know you must be nearby. Show yourself."

Hesitantly, Wily slid open the secret door that connected the maintenance passage to the study and took small steps into the chilly room.

Odette, Moshul, and Pryvyd turned to look at Wily, but he kept his face hidden in the shadows.

"Moshul," Pryvyd said, "the fireflies."

The earth giant held out its hand, and a group of flying bugs lifted from his palm. As the bugs flapped their wings, their backsides began to light up. They were bright enough to light the entire room, Wily included.

"Who is this?" Pryvyd asked, as his face twisted in confusion.

"My trapsmith," Stalag wheezed from the floor. "His name is Snare."

"Wily Snare," Wily clarified.

"But this is just a human boy," Odette said as she surveyed him from head to toe.

"Actually, I'm a hobgoblet," Wily countered.

Odette didn't seem to need a second glance.

"I think I know a human when I see one," she said.

Wily looked down at his smooth-skinned hands. It was humiliating. He was such an ugly hobgoblet she mistook him for a human!

"Certainly this is not the trapsmith who is responsible for devising the traps of Carrion Tomb," Pryvyd said.

"He is the one and only," Stalag grumbled.

"From the way the Oracle of Oak described him, I expected him to be older," Odette said to Pryvyd. "An ancient squatling or an elder locksage."

"I think the cavern mage is trying to fool us," Pryvyd replied.

"He was just a child when I received him," Stalag interjected. "Barely able to walk."

Wily wondered if suddenly Stalag had grown confused. He spoke up.

"Received me? I thought my parents worked here and were killed by thieves."

Stalag looked startled, as if he'd dropped a bagful of snakes and now had to somehow convince them all to slither back inside. Instead of responding to Wily, Stalag turned back to the invaders.

"How can we be sure this is not merely a common kitchen boy?" Pryvyd asked, still holding his sword in place.

"He doesn't look like much, I know," Stalag said. "But he has talented fingers and a clever mind."

Wily had never heard the cavern mage speak highly of him (or anyone other than himself, for that matter).

Odette walked up to Wily and looked him directly in the eyes. She held her stare for a long time as if his eyeballs and lashes held secrets that could be revealed by a strong gaze. Wily swallowed hard and his throat became very dry. He wondered what she was thinking.

Then Odette reached into her pouch and pulled out a small wooden box.

"Open this," she said, shoving the box into his hands.

Wily looked down at the object he had just been given. There was a simple copper latch on one side and a set of hinges on the other. An eager hobgoblet might just unhook the latch and snap it open. Not Wily, though. He never opened anything without proper examination.

He flipped the box over and ran his fingernail along the back. As he had thought, there was a pin-size hole hidden in a dark knot of the wood. He reached into his trapsmith belt and pulled out a screwdriver barely as thick as a ghost-spider bristle. It was just the right size. He stuck the tool into the indentation and twisted it. There was a soft *click* inside. Wily opened the box. It was empty.

Odette snatched the box back from him and shut it, then slipped it into the satchel that hung from her shoulder.

"He's the trapsmith," she said aloud, before turning back to the cavern mage, who was still pinned to the ground by Moshul and Righteous.

"Hold out your wrists," she commanded Stalag.

Stalag reluctantly did as she asked. Odette pulled two sets of glowing shackles from her satchel and bound his wrists and ankles to each other. Moshul and Pryvyd released Stalag, who now was unable to stand or even crawl.

"Get to work," Odette said as she tossed her silent giant companion her shoulder satchel.

Moshul walked over to the vault and opened the silk bag. The moss giant grabbed a huge fistful of gold and shoved it into the open pouch. Then grabbed another. And another. But even after ten huge heaps of precious metal, the bag didn't seem any heavier than the moment the giant had opened it.

"An everstuff satchel?" Stalag groaned.

"We're emptying the vault," Pryvyd grinned. "If it can fit through the mouth of that bag, it's coming with us."

Stalag looked on in horror as one priceless piece of treasure after another disappeared into the bag.

"That's decades of hoarding," he moaned.

"Consider it spring-cleaning," Pryvyd said.

Odette turned back to Wily. "You are leaving with us."

"Leave?" Wily said. "And go where?"

"Out of Carrion Tomb," Odette said as if it were the most natural thing in the world.

She can't be serious. He was a hobgoblet. He couldn't go—

"You're going to take me into the Above?" Wily asked, his panic tinged with a strange thrill.

"If that's what you call everything outside this dungeon," Pryvyd answered, "then, yes."

This was everything Wily had wanted—but he couldn't leave. There was a giant burning reason he had to stay in Carrion Tomb for the rest of his life.

"I'll die if I go to the Above," Wily spoke with trembling lips. "I'm a hobgoblet. My skin—I'll need something to protect it from melting."

Odette looked at him oddly, trying hard to restrain a laugh.

"First of all, you're not a hobgoblet," Odette said. "And second, hobgoblets are not made out of butter."

Wily twisted his mouth, confused. There was so much wrong with what she was saying.

Seeing the look on Wily's face, Pryvyd stepped forward.

"Hobgoblets can go in the sun," the knight explained. "I've seen it with my own eyes."

Wily had to take a moment to process this. *If that is true, then . . . how many lies has Stalag told me? Could I really have stepped into the Above any time I wished to?*

By this point, Moshul had cleared out almost the entire vault; only a large wooden chest and a pair of jade thrones were left. The giant was attempting unsuccessfully to cram an enormous silver platter into the bag.

"Leave it," Odette ordered him. "I don't want you ripping the satchel."

With a shrug, Moshul tossed the platter onto the ground.

"Show us the quickest way out of the tomb," Odette said to Wily as she brushed her strange-colored hair from her eyes. "We need to be far away when Stalag breaks free from those enchanted shackles."

Wily had to make a quick decision. He could try to lead the invaders into a trap or aid them in their escape and his own. . . . *Or is this a kidnapping rather than an escape? Can I trust them?* One thing was for certain: he certainly didn't trust his "father" anymore—Stalag had lied about his parents. Wily had despised Stalag before, but now fury burned through his chest.

I could help them escape. I could escape. Even as he said it in his head, it felt right.

"We can take the maintenance tunnels, but it might be tight for the giant," Wily said.

Moshul made a series of angry hand motions.

"Moshul is a moss golem," Odette clarified, "and doesn't like to be called otherwise. Giants are oafish creatures who like only to break things and chew their toenails."

"Lead the way," Pryvyd said. "Moshul will squeeze if he has to."

"Don't go," Stalag called out from the floor. "You belong here. Things will be different."

Wily looked upon his master, who was hiding his usual cruelty behind a mask of kindness. He could see straight through his lies.

"Make your own traps," Wily said, talking back to

his "father" for the first time. It was an exhilarating thrill. Wily turned to the others. "Follow me."

Leaving Stalag behind, struggling and bemoaning the loss of his treasures, Pryvyd, Righteous, Odette, and Moshul followed Wily through the secret door into the maintenance tunnel.

"I don't understand," Wily said as he hurried them down the side tunnel. "Why do you want me?"

"We asked the Oracle of Oak where we could find a trapsmith who would help us on our mission," Odette said. "Her magic acorns sent us to Carrion Tomb."

"Mission?" Wily asked, totally confused. "What mission?"

Odette, Pryvyd, and Moshul all looked at each other as if the answer was perfectly obvious.

"Raiding dungeons for treasure," Pryvyd said.

"If you can make traps, you'll be able to break them, too," Odette stated. "Your skills will be very helpful when we sneak into the Catacombs of Blood. And Vileo's Maze. And Squalor Keep."

"Are you saying a prophet told you to come find me?" Wily asked.

"The Oracle of Oak is considered by many to be the greatest seer in the land," Odette said. "Although after meeting you, I'm wondering if she had one too many acorns drop on her head."

In a daze, Wily led Odette, Moshul, and Pryvyd to the tunnel outside the prison chamber where the oglodytes were still waiting.

"Whash going on?" a large oglodyte guard yelled as she slammed the end of her trident on the ground. "They can't be in here!"

Before Wily could speak, Odette turned to the oglodyte.

"We made it to Stalag," she said, "and we grovblundered him."

This left the oglodytes speechless. *Grovblundered* was another of the many words that the oglodytes used for ambush—and hardly anybody who wasn't an oglodyte would have known this one. It meant to "surprise, humiliate, and force into a whimpering surrender."

The guards looked to Wily, their eyes asking if this had actually happened the way she described.

"It's true," Wily said, almost too flustered to speak.

The oglodytes' faces turned a darker green than normal and their eyes widened. Nobody had ever grovblundered Stalag.

"Stalag offered us safe passage out of the tomb in exchange for our mercy," Odette lied.

"That doesn't shound like him to me," the slimy oglodyte said. "We'll have to go invesh-it-tigate ourselves."

Wily looked over to see Moshul make a few quick hand gestures to Pryvyd.

"If you think you can," Pryvyd said to Moshul, "be my guest."

"Why's it moving its fingers all funny and the like?" the club-wielding oglodyte asked.

Moshul swiftly grabbed the guards in his large earthen hands and smashed their heads together. They both slid to the ground, unconscious.

"We need to move fast before the rest of the guards show up," Odette said to Wily.

"This way," he said as he took off.

Turning from the main dungeon, he led his new companions through the residence quarters. They moved past the dining hall, where Wily sniffed the musty and familiar odor of yeast cakes being baked in the lava ovens.

As they ran past the salvage room, Wily caught a glimpse of his equipment wagon and a couple of fearful hobgoblets hiding behind it. Approaching his own room, Wily eyed the picture of the hammer above his door handle and knew at once that this would be the last time he ever saw it. For a moment, he thought about racing into his room and grabbing his precious stash of books, but he knew he didn't have time. At least he had the gwarf's journal still shoved in his trapsmith belt.

"Wily!"

Looking down the hall, Wily spied Roveeka trundling toward them. Pryvyd pulled out his weapon.

"Put your sword away," Wily said to Pryvyd. "That's my sister."

"What's going on?" Roveeka asked.

"I'm leaving the dungeon," Wily said, the words popping out on their own.

It took a few seconds for this statement to really hit Roveeka. Then her face fell, like a stone sinking to the bottom of a pool. She looked down at her feet.

"I'm going to miss you," Roveeka said sadly.

He would miss her, too. Unless—

"You can come with us," Wily blurted. "Hobgoblets don't melt in the sun. Stalag lied. He lied about everything. You'll be just fine."

Roveeka raised her head with a big (albeit crooked) smile on her face.

"No," Odette said quickly, "she absolutely cannot."

"She's the only family I have," Wily replied. "I can't leave her behind."

Odette eyed Roveeka and clearly didn't seem impressed.

"You didn't think much of me at first glance," Wily continued, and then offered: "She's a very talented knife tosser."

"And she'd be safer here," Odette countered.

"Do you want me to cooperate?" Wily asked with arms crossed.

"Not if it means bringing her," Odette said.

"If she can leave now," Pryvyd said impatiently, "I'd say yes."

Moshul was nodding, too.

The screams of oglodytes could be heard echoing from deep within the tomb.

"Fine," Odette relented. "But we need to move."

"Should I bring a change of clothes?" Roveeka asked with a twitch of her droopy eye.

Odette looked as if she were already regretting her decision.

"No time for that," Wily said gently.

"That's okay," Roveeka replied brightly. "I've got all I need. Mum, Pops, and you."

Just then the shrieking stones began to wail.

"That can't be good," Pryvyd said.

"It isn't," Wily answered. "Stalag's going to try to shut us in."

Wily took off down the corridor and the others sprinted behind. After only a few strides, Roveeka was lagging.

"She better be a good knife tosser," Odette snapped at Wily, "because speed certainly isn't her gift."

"Moshul," Pryvyd shouted, "can you lend the hobgoblet a hand?"

The moss golem reached back, grabbed Roveeka, and tucked her into the crook of his arm.

"Wheee!" Roveeka squealed like a child getting her first giant scorpion ride.

Leaving the residence quarters behind, Wily led them up a narrow set of steps. Every step closer to the entrance corridor made Wily's whole body pulse with excitement. For a lifetime, he had waited for this.

He looked over his shoulder to see that Moshul's large body filled the entire width of the passage. The earth golem's mossy arms roughly rubbed against the walls, creating a trail of greenery in his wake.

The steps wound their way up to the secret entrance to the Temple of Foreboding. Wily flipped a lever, and the stone column along the east wall of the large room opened. They passed through it into the first room of

Carrion Tomb where the Knights of the Golden Sun still lay sleeping on the floor.

"Stop where you are," yelled an oglodyte standing at a doorway opposite the entrance corridor.

Behind the oglodyte were a dozen bone soldiers, living skeletons of bone and cartilage, each one holding a sword in its skeletal hand. The bone soldiers were mindless, but foolishly loyal.

Wily and the others didn't stop. He ran for the Archway of Many Eyes as his trapsmith belt shook and rattled against his waist.

"Get them!" the oglodyte commanded the living skeletons. "Hold them until Stalag arrives."

"We can't outrun the skeletons," Wily said. "Being nothing but bone makes them quite speedy."

"Then we'll face them in combat," Pryvyd said, pulling his blade with his hovering arm and raising his spiked shield with the other.

"No!" Wily shouted. "Just keep going."

Wily broke off from the group and ran for the statue of Glothmurk. The bone soldiers sprinted after him, their heels and toes clattering against the stone floor.

"Turn back or be crushed by the might of Glothmurk," the idol said in its deep bubbling voice as it raised a tentacle.

"That's what I'm hoping," Wily whispered to himself.

Wily stepped onto the pressure plate in the ground. RUMBLE. Out from the wall, the giant boulder came rolling, just missing Wily. It struck the skeletons, shattering some and sending the others flying.

"At least I won't be the one stuck pushing that boulder back in place," Wily said with a grin.

With Odette taking the lead, they ran up the long entrance corridor that led to the mouth of the dungeon. At the fifty stride mark, Wily spied a thin line of dirt on the ground. It would not have seemed like much to anyone else, but for Wily, it was a spot of great meaning. When he swept the dungeon floor, he pushed the dirt and mud to this point but never beyond. This was the farthest he had ever traveled toward the exit of Carrion Tomb. It was a line he had never dared cross on his own, but today he would. Behind them, Wily could hear the sound of oglodytes shouting and gristle hounds growling.

As the tunnel began to slope steeper and the air lost its pleasant mustiness, Wily's palms began to sweat. *That's strange. My palms only sweat when I'm nervous. I should be excited, not frightened. The Above is . . .*

As they came around a bend, Wily could see a circle of the same strange color as Odette's hair, only even more intense, in the distance. With every step, the circle grew bigger and bigger.

. . . terrifying. What am I doing? I've made a terrible mistake. I've gotten carried away by the possibility of it all. What if Stalag didn't lie? Maybe he and Roveeka were about to liquefy into a puddle of ooze.

"I can't," Wily said as he stopped suddenly in the entrance corridor. "I don't want to melt."

"Stop being ridiculous!" Odette yelled as she grabbed his wrist.

Odette tried to tug Wily forward, but he refused to move.

"Moshul," Odette shouted, "a little help here."

Wily felt himself being scooped up from behind. There was no stopping his inevitable end now. Moshul was pushing him toward the exit.

A blast of powerful light smashed into Wily's eyes. His pupils shrank so quickly it hurt. It was like a thousand torches had been lit all at once and thrust toward him.

He closed his eyes as he was shoved into the blinding brightness of the Above.

6

THE HORRIBLE,
TERRIBLE ABOVE

His whole body was awash in light and warmth.

And he was alive.

And he was in no pain.

Am I really in the Above? Or am I still under the protection of the tomb's thick stone roof?

With his eyes shut, Wily ran his fingers along his cheeks to make sure they were still there. He was relieved to find they felt the same as they always did: smooth, with the faintest prickle of hair along his jaw. His fingers moved to the burn mark on his arm. It, too, felt unchanged.

Wily heard a mighty smash behind him as the ground beneath his feet shook.

"You're all right," Pryvyd said. "You can open your eyes."

Wily peeled his lids open. It took a moment for his eyes to adjust. He immediately looked down at his arms. They were neither on fire or turning to jelly the way Stalag had warned him they would. It was another falsehood that the cavern mage had hammered into his head.

As Wily looked up, the world around him came into focus. Gray boulders surrounded Wily and the others. Behind them was the entrance to Carrion Tomb, which was now blocked by a large rock placed there by Moshul. Roveeka stood nearby, smiling.

"I didn't melt," Roveeka said. "At least, not yet."

Perhaps the Above isn't so different after all?

Then Wily looked up, and terror took hold of him once more: there was no roof over him, only an endless void. He dropped low to the ground as if he might accidentally fall upward.

"What is that?" Wily asked with awe and fear.

"The sky," Pryvyd answered. "Have you never seen it before?"

Wily shook his head.

"And that color?" Wily asked, still staring upward.

"It's called blue."

Blue. It made even the most vibrant shade of gray

look dull by comparison. The same bold and beautiful color as Odette's hair. Before today, he might have seen this color once or twice before, but only ever in its faintest form. The tinge of blue when a torch slowly extinguishes to black. Or a hint of blue reflecting quietly in the heart of a newly mined diamond. He had never seen it like this. Wily was spellbound.

"The blue is very big," Roveeka said simply.

Moshul threw another giant rock in front of the entrance to Carrion Tomb to make sure that Stalag and the oglodytes would not be able to come after them as quickly.

Ahead, Odette disappeared, having moved between a pair of boulders. Wily followed after her.

As he rounded the corner, he spotted something that made him leap backward.

In the next circle of high stones was the very same object that he had seen sketched in the gwarf's journal: a large hand reaching out of the ground with fingers sprouting more fingers. And it was green. He scrambled away before it could grab hold of him.

But the hand remained still.

Wily looked again at the object and realized it was not a hand at all, but some sort of plant. A few leaves were sprouting from the "fingers." Wily stepped over to the object and touched its coarse outer skin.

"You're going to be seeing a lot more trees," Odette said with a sigh. "I hope you don't plan on hugging every one of them."

Pryvyd took Wily by the arm and guided him around the next boulder to the wide-open mountainside, and Roveeka stepped up behind him. There was nothing here to block their view.

"Breathe it in," Pryvyd said gently. "Let the splendor fill your lungs."

Wily's jaw dropped. The sight would have been breathtaking for someone who had lived their entire life in the Above. For Wily, it was nothing short of mind-expanding.

Down the slope, he could see hundreds of thousands of trees, their arms as green as giant-slug slime. They stood tall like spikes hidden beneath a trapdoor. They sprouted in every direction as far as Wily could see and, he imagined, much farther beyond. To his left, there were jagged mountains that scratched the blue sky with their white crowns. Ahead, in the distance, a long, thin river cut a path through the cluster of trees; its water rushed swiftly, making splashes of white as it flowed over the rocks. To the right, the trees stretched off into rolling hills of dense gray smoke.

Wily's attention was drawn back to the sky as a flock

of colorful batlike creatures flew overhead. Roveeka saw them, too.

"What are those?" she asked.

"Birds," Pryvyd said.

Roveeka repeated the word back slowly and incorrectly. "Birks."

"Where are the walls that hold the sky up?" Wily said quietly, almost to himself.

"That's a silly question," Roveeka said with a laugh. "They're invisible, of course."

"We got a lot to teach you, kid," Pryvyd said.

Righteous clapped Wily on the shoulder and gave him a squeeze.

Two tall creatures that resembled giant hounds with hoofed feet and long snouts were tied to a tree downhill.

"We should get as far away from here as possible," Odette said. "It won't take much magic to crack those boulders."

She hurried toward one of the large beasts as her blue hair fluttered gently in the breeze. Then she leaped atop its back.

Wily took one more look at the wide expanse before him. The Above was more beautiful than he could have ever dreamed. It was all so new, and yet Wily had the strange feeling that this was where he was meant to be.

"Come now," Pryvyd said. "There's a lot more of Panthasos to see."

"Panthasos?" Wily asked. It was a word he had never heard before.

"It's the name of the kingdom you've been living in," Pryvyd answered. "No one calls it the Above up here."

Wily repeated the three-syllable word in his head. He had spent his whole life in a place whose name he had never known.

"You'll be riding on my horse," Pryvyd said, beckoning him.

Wily looked at the strange four-legged beast with caution. He eyed its square snout and toeless feet. The horse snorted ominously.

"Actually," Wily said, stepping away, "I'd rather walk if it's just the same."

"Unacceptable," Odette said sternly. "We need to move, and move fast."

Pryvyd raised a hand to Odette, quieting her. The knight turned back to Wily.

"I understand the horse looks a bit imposing," Pryvyd said quietly, "but he's a kind creature."

Pryvyd ran his fingers down the creature's neck and along his back.

"Later, you can even feed him an apple."

Wily considered, then asked—

"What's an apple?"

Odette let out a huff.

"This is ridiculous. Get on the horse," Odette demanded.

Pryvyd reached out a hand to Wily, who approached cautiously. The knight hoisted him up onto the back of his strange riding beast. Although Wily felt a bit unstable being so high off the ground, it was not nearly as scary as he'd thought it would be. In fact, he liked how the horse's hairy bristles tickled his ankles.

Odette eyed Wily with impatience before nudging her horse forward. Wily was glad to be riding with Pryvyd and not stuck pressed up against Odette.

As Pryvyd's horse began to trot downhill, Wily took one last look at the entrance to Carrion Tomb.

"What about me?" Roveeka yelled as the two horses left her behind.

"You get the seat with the view," Odette said, calling back.

"I don't underst—"

Moshul's giant hand grabbed Roveeka and lifted her onto his large mossy shoulders.

She wrapped her fingers around the giant's neck as he took long strides. Wily turned back and saw that his sister had a huge smile on her face, and for the first time, it didn't seem crooked at all.

WILY WAS SO busy studying the fireless white clumps of smoke drifting through the blue sky that he didn't notice a flying creature land on his arm. When he spotted it, he let out a scream of terror and nearly jumped off Pryvyd's horse.

Odette spun around with alarm. Pryvyd pulled his horse to a sharp stop. Righteous tore his sword from Pryvyd's sheath.

"What did you see?" Odette questioned sharply, scanning the dense woods. "A slither troll? Frakdragons? *Gearfolk?*"

"On my arm," Wily whispered, staring at the orange-and-black winged insect standing fearlessly on his elbow.

Pryvyd looked down at Wily's arm. He slipped his sword away.

"No danger here," Pryvyd called out to Odette and Moshul. "Just a butterfly."

With the back of his hand, Pryvyd swatted away the insect. Wily let out a sigh of relief, and then looked over to see Odette giving him a withering stare.

"It looked poisonous," Wily said, embarrassed, his cheeks warming.

"There's plenty to be frightened of in Panthasos," Odette said, "but unless you're a puddle of sugar water, I think you're going to survive a vicious butterfly attack."

Odette turned back to the road ahead. As she did, Wily thought he saw the corners of her mouth upturn into a smirk.

Nearby, the butterfly had fluttered to a white flower and landed on a petal. Wily kept his eye on it warily as Pryvyd gave their mount a gentle nudge with the heel of his boot, urging it forward.

"If it's not meant to harm, then why was it placed here?" Wily asked Pryvyd.

"Placed?" Pryvyd replied. "I'm not sure what you mean."

"I'm saying, why was the butterfly put here in this tree tunnel?" Wily continued. "What is its purpose?"

"No one placed it in these woods," Pryvyd explained

as the horses continued on their way. "It's part of nature. It's free to do what it wants."

The idea was so puzzling to Wily that he could barely make sense of it.

"How strange," Wily mumbled, lost in thought. "In the tomb, everything has a purpose . . . mostly to squash, catch, or swallow invaders."

"It's different up here," Pryvyd said as a flock of birds winged overhead. He gestured to the yellow-bellied creatures as they weaved through the air, screeching and whistling their haunting calls. "Like all wild creatures, the sparrows have no master and no bounds."

"It sounds very disorganized to me," Wily said as their horse clopped down the muddy path.

From just behind, Wily heard a sound that he had rarely heard before. It was Roveeka laughing. (There was very little funny about Carrion Tomb, and even less worth laughing about.) He turned to see that she, still sitting high atop Moshul's shoulders, was being tickled by furry leaves on thin branches that brushed across her arms and face.

"You've got to try this, Wily," Roveeka yelled down. "So much fun!"

Unlike his half sister, Wily was not enjoying himself.

A life of living inside a trap-filled tomb had made Wily suspicious of everything. He couldn't help eyeing the dirt ground for pressure plates and the trees for hidden blowguns. When a hard spiky object fell from a nearby branch, Wily instinctively prepared to defend himself in case more dropped from overhead.

Odette looked over at Wily as he pulled Pryvyd's spiked shield over his head.

"Please don't scream again," Odette said. "We don't need everyone in Rivergate Woods knowing we're here."

"It could be an ambush," Wily said, peeking out from behind the shield.

"It was a pinecone," Odette replied.

Wily looked up at the tree branches skeptically.

"And are pinecones safe?" Wily questioned. "I was always taught, if something moves and you don't know what it is . . . it's probably trying to kill you."

"Wow," Odette said. "You're completely paranoid."

"Thank you," Wily responded, taking Odette's insult as a compliment.

"That's not a good thing," Odette clarified.

"Paranoia is one of the keys to survival," Wily countered. "The day you stop being overly cautious is the day you become a between-meals snack for a giant shade nibbler."

"That's a famous story," Roveeka chimed in from her high perch on Moshul's shoulders.

"A famous *true* story," added Wily, "with a not-so-happy ending for both the careless oglodyte and the shade nibbler who choked on the oglodyte's trident. And it has a very important moral that every smart hobgoblet heeds. Not everything is out to get you; just most things."

"But you're not a hobgoblet," Odette retorted.

Now Wily was mad. This elf girl he barely knew was telling him what he was. *What does she know? Nothing. I know what I am. A hobgoblet. A very unusual hobgoblet, for sure. But certainly not a human being. They are hairy, flat-faced invaders whose only goal in life is taking stuff that doesn't belong to them.*

"Don't be cruel," Pryvyd said to Odette.

"It's like he's never looked in a mirror," Odette replied, exasperated.

"What's a mirror?" Wily asked timidly.

"Shiny thing that you can see your own reflection in," Pryvyd answered. "And if you're like Odette, it sucks away hours of your life."

"Elves like to keep up their appearances," Odette said as she ran her fingers through her sky-blue bangs. "You might want to spend a little more time in front of one. You're filthy."

"I don't think the gearfolk are going to care if I have a bit of dirt on my cheeks," Pryvyd said.

Odette turned her attention back to Wily.

"Tell me you never caught a glimpse of yourself in a well-shined shield," Odette questioned. "You and your half sister look nothing alike."

Wily felt his cheeks redden with anger.

"That's because I'm a girl and he's a boy," Roveeka chimed in from Moshul's shoulders.

That hardly explained their difference in appearance, but Wily appreciated Roveeka sticking up for him.

"Go easy on him," Pryvyd said quietly to Odette out of the corner of his mouth. "Remember the boy is going to have our lives in his hands when he's disarming the traps in the dungeons."

"His name is Wily," Roveeka yelled down. (A hobgoblet's pointy ears are very attuned to whispers.) "Not 'the boy.'"

Just then, a loud shatter broke their conversation. Wily spun around to see if he could spot the source of the distant sound. All he could tell was that the noise came from behind them, far up the mountain.

"Moshul," Odette called out to the lumbering moss golem, "check to see if that's what I think it is."

Behind Wily, Moshul came to a stop. He bent down

and put the side of his head to the ground, like he did back in the Fountain Room. Roveeka nearly fell off as she tightened her arms around his neck.

"What's he doing?" Roveeka asked.

"He's one with the earth," Odette answered. "He can hear the vibrations in the mud and the stone. They tell him things that others can't hear."

After a long listen, Moshul lifted his head once more. He turned to Odette and Pryvyd and moved his large hands in strange patterns.

"Why does he make those odd gestures?" Roveeka asked.

"As you may have noticed," Odette shot back, "Moshul doesn't have a mouth."

"He can hear what we say, but the only way he can talk is by using his hands. It's called sign language," Pryvyd explained.

Wily watched the golem's fingers dance through the air, but they were just as confusing as the scribbles on the pages of his books.

"The boulder in front of Carrion Tomb has been broken," Odette translated. "Moshul can hear the footsteps of the cavern mage, six oglodytes, and three giant scorpions."

"That's bad," Wily worried aloud. "The scorpions

can move very quickly. Stalag and the oglodytes will use them as steeds. They'll be much faster than the four-legged riding beasts we're traveling on."

"We've got a good head start on them," Pryvyd said calmly. "Hopefully, we can lose them in the dim light of the woods ahead."

"That doesn't sound like the best idea either," Wily replied. "Oglodytes are extremely talented hunters in the dark. We should stay in brightly lit places. The light hinders their ability to react quickly. It will be our only chance."

"Just one problem with that," Odette interjected. "In about four hours, everything will be dark. There's this little thing we have out here in the Above: it's called 'night.'"

"Well . . . ," Wily said, thinking, "is there any way we could delay it?"

From the looks on Odette's and Pryvyd's faces, Wily could tell that the answer was no.

7

UP RIVER, DOWN RIVER

A short while later, the horses emerged from the woods, arriving at a swiftly moving river. It was not, however, made of lava like the ones populating the lower tunnels of the tomb. This river was composed of only sparkling blue water that shimmered brightly in the sunlight.

Odette dismounted her steed and led it to the water's edge.

"Off you go," Pryvyd said to Wily, helping him down from the horse.

The moss golem removed Roveeka from his back and walked into the middle of the river. He stuck both his arms deep into the water. At once, his entire body of dry earth, partially hidden beneath a scattering of moss, turned from a pale tan to a dark brown. The vegetation that covered him from head to heel quivered as if delighted. A row of magenta mushrooms sprouted from his shoulders where there had been none before.

"You should get a drink, too," Pryvyd said to Wily. "I can see your lips are dry."

Despite Wily being parched, he felt very uncertain about the safety of the water. He spied a few fish swimming by the shore. Perhaps they were actually thirsty travelers who had been transformed by the cursed river? But the back of his throat was starting to get as scratchy as a bristle mole's rear end. After watching Odette take a few gulps and remain an elf, Wily decided to risk a drink.

He bent down next to the riverbed. He cupped his hands and brought a scoop of water to his lips. He was surprised by its gentle taste. It was so different from the chalky and bland water that he collected from the dripping stalactites of Carrion Tomb. After a single gulp of cave water, it felt like your tongue was caked with mud. But not this. This water was clear and cool and refreshing.

"Blech!" Roveeka said, nearly gagging on her swallow. "It's all slippery."

Roveeka dove into her snacking pouch, pulled out a dried insect, and popped it in her mouth.

"Does anyone need a cricket to wash away the taste?" Roveeka offered.

Pryvyd shook his head politely.

"They're very flavorful and crunchy," Roveeka continued.

"I'm sure it must be delicious," Odette said with a smirk, ". . . for a hobgoblet. I'm going to pass."

It is extremely unwise to question a hobgoblet's palate.

"Hobgoblets have the most refined sense of taste of any creature," Roveeka said, sticking out her long black tongue as proof. "We can taste a single grain of salt in a cauldron of dragon drool."

"The better question is why are you tasting dragon drool?" Odette replied.

"How else do you make maggot stew?" Roveeka asked.

"That's repulsive." Odette grimaced.

Roveeka narrowed her eyes in anger. She pulled Mum and Pops out of her waistband and started for Odette.

"Take that back," Roveeka demanded.

Before Roveeka got within grabbing distance, Righteous came between them. His bronze gauntlet stopped Roveeka in her tracks.

Pryvyd looked over from the rock he was leaning against.

"Mind your own business," he said to Righteous. "Breaking up a fight? That seems like something I would have done. Back when I cared about that sort of thing."

With a gentle push, Righteous nudged Roveeka away from Odette. Then Wily watched as Righteous floated over to groom the horse.

"Did your arm really do that on its own?" Wily asked the reclining knight.

"It's got a mind of its own," Pryvyd said. "Righteous abides by the foolish principles of the Knights of the Golden Sun. It still thinks it's a hero's arm. Not a disillusioned thief's who knows there's no place for heroes in Panthasos anymore."

Pryvyd shouted over to Righteous, "You think you're better than me?"

The hovering arm shot back a thumbs-up.

"See if I scratch your elbow when you have an itch," Pryvyd shot back. He taunted Righteous by wiggling the fingers on his left hand.

Just then, Moshul came up behind Odette and gently tapped her on the shoulder.

"What is it?" she asked.

The moss golem began signing to his companion. As he did, her eyes widened in alarm.

"Already?" Odette said. "They're moving faster than I had expected."

Odette turned to the others.

"Stalag and his oglodytes are only a mile or so behind us."

She didn't need to say it twice. Pryvyd hurried to his horse as Moshul scooped Roveeka up in his palm.

"If we take to the river," Pryvyd thought aloud, "they won't be able to follow our footprints. They'll be forced to toss a coin to decide which direction to go in. Upriver or downriver."

"We'll have to hope they pick the wrong way," Odette replied.

"I have a better idea," Wily interjected. "What if we take neither way?"

Everyone turned to Wily.

"As a trapsmith," he continued, "I had to make it look like each new invader was the first in years to stumble into the tomb."

"Where are you going with this?" Odette said impatiently, before launching into a backflip and landing neatly on her horse.

"A haunted library doesn't seem scary if it looks like someone else just walked through the day before." Wily elaborated, "I would walk the corridors, sprinkling dust on everything to cover up footprints. Perhaps we can do the same."

Odette looked over to Pryvyd and Moshul to see what they thought of the idea.

"It's worth a try," Pryvyd said.

Moshul nodded in agreement.

"Cleaning up after sloppy adventurers is one of my specialties," Wily offered.

"Okay, dungeon boy," Odette said with a sigh. "Let's find out just how tidy you can be."

"THEEESH FOOT-TA-PRINTS END at the water," Agorop called out as he peered over the head of the scorpion he was riding.

Three oglodytes on foot were doing their own investigating, stabbing the underbrush with their tridents.

"Weez not finding any-a-thing here neither," a burly

oglodyte with an eye patch said, kicking a clump of tall grass with his webbed toes.

"Check the other side of the river," Stalag commanded from his perch on the back of the largest scorpion.

His bony finger pointed across the water, trembling menacingly as if it might fire off a crackling arrow of energy at any second.

"Ab-sho-tively, Lord Shtal-ag," Sceely said, snapping the reins of her riding scorpion.

The dagger-sharp claws at the end of her mount's eight legs rattled the loose rocks along the riverbank as they splashed into the water.

Just up the hill, hiding in a foul-smelling turnip-berry bush, Wily and Odette watched the oglodytes and scorpions search for them. Wily had, only moments before their pursuers arrived, finished hiding the last of their tracks. Pryvyd, Righteous, Moshul, Roveeka, and the horses were already hiding deep in the woods, far out of sight of the river.

"Let's just go now," Odette said, "before they get any closer."

"The scorpions," Wily explained, "can spot even the tiniest motion a hundred strides away, but if we stay still, we should be completely invisible to them."

"And what about the oglodytes?" Odette asked. "We won't be invisible to them."

"I never said it was a perfect plan," Wily said, swallowing nervously.

Odette looked like she wanted to poke Wily in the eye. Fortunately, she was able to restrain herself.

"I don't shee anything over here," Sceely shouted from the far side of the river as her scorpion used its large pincer to pick up a log and snap it in half.

More pressing was the giant scorpion with Agorop on top. It was making its way up the hill to the turnip-berry bush. Odette grabbed Wily's hand, encouraging him to bolt, but he squeezed her back hard.

"Just freeze," Wily said between clenched teeth.

He knew if they moved even a muscle, the hyper-sensitive predator would realize they were there. All they could do was remain completely still.

As the creature grew closer, Wily held his breath so as not to move even his chest. He had watched what they would do to their prey during feeding time. He most certainly did not want the same thing to happen to him.

One of the scorpion's front legs was now nearly touching the turnipberry bush where Odette and Wily were huddled together.

"What is it, girl?" Agorop said through his rows of jagged gnashers. "You find something?"

The scorpion began to poke at the bush with its claw-tipped foreleg. Wily could feel Odette squeezing his hand so hard he was wondering if she would break it.

Suddenly, the tail of the arachnid shot toward them. The stinger plunged into the bush. It happened so fast Wily didn't even have time to leap backward.

The poisonous stinger found its mark, plunging deep into the fleshy back . . . of a furry toad. It pulled the amphibian out of the turnipberry bush. The toad's limp tongue brushed right across Wily's cheek, leaving a sticky, wet mark.

"Is it the boy?" Stalag hissed with wicked pleasure.

Agorop eyed the captured prey as the scorpion pulled its tail from the shrub.

"No," Agorop said, disappointed. "Just a toad."

The scorpion shoved the dead amphibian between its clicking mandibles and began to chew.

As the scorpion and oglodyte rider headed back for the river, Odette relaxed her grip on Wily's hand. She looked down and suddenly realized whose hand she had been holding. As soon as the scorpions were a safe distance away, she snatched her hand away from Wily's.

"Whash your wish, Lord Shtal-ag?" Sceely called

out as her scorpion searched the tree line for a meal of its own. "Shall we go up-da river or down-da river?"

"We'll split up and go both ways," Stalag hissed, pulling his hood over his head to block the sunlight. "They couldn't have gotten far."

Stalag and his hunting party divided in two, each group following the river in opposite directions.

"I knew your trapsmithing skills would come in handy," Odette whispered to Wily. "I never expected your maid skills to be helpful as well."

Odette turned and began to scramble up the hill in the direction of where Pryvyd, Moshul, and Roveeka were hiding with the horses. Wily smiled and scampered after her.

As they reached the top of the rise, Pryvyd called out from behind a cluster of trees.

"Did they take the bait?"

"They sure did," Odette said. "But the farther away we are when they discover they've been tricked the better."

Odette pushed through the shrubs and bounded onto her horse. She was already a hundred steps ahead before Wily and Pryvyd had mounted their own horse.

"She would never admit it," Pryvyd said quietly to Wily, "but I think you impressed her."

As the group took the twisting high road out of Rivergate Woods, Wily was treated to an amazing sight: the sky was transforming with a magic more powerful than any spell he had ever seen cast before. This was an illusion of an epic scale, one that even the great Stalag would be incapable of conjuring.

The blue sky was turning the color of lava, and centipede bellies, and ruby dust. Even the clouds suddenly appeared to be awash with dark purple oglodyte blood. It was as if the roof of a cave had suddenly been painted by invisible brushes.

It took Wily's breath away.

"It's called a sunset," Odette said from her neighboring horse.

How lucky, Wily thought. *I happened out of the dungeon on the very day the sun set.*

He stared up at the sky until all the colors faded to gray.

8

MORNING ELF

Wily rolled over and tried burying his face in the cloth bundle he had been using as a pillow. It had been a tough sleep. He was accustomed to sleeping in pitch-blackness, and the moon and stars had been so bright that he had felt their light shining through his shut lids all night long. Now with dawn coming, keeping his eyes closed seemed impossible.

"You hungry?" Pryvyd called out to Wily.

Wily looked over to see Pryvyd holding a long skewer of orange mushrooms over a small crackling fire.

"Actually," Wily said as he pulled a thin blanket off his legs, "I am."

Crossing through the small campsite, Wily passed

Odette and Roveeka, who were still quietly sleeping. Moshul, who had no need for rest, had spent the evening on the slight rise, scanning the tree line and rocky crevices for unwelcome visitors. Righteous circled the camp, holding the knight's blade vigilantly in a clutched fist, ready to defend the group if the need presented itself.

Wily approached Pryvyd, who was reclining against a tree stump. The knight had removed his bronze armor for the evening, and Wily couldn't help but think that he looked much less imposing without his chest plate. Pryvyd didn't have the bulging muscles of a gwarven warrior or the tough skin of a slither troll.

Wily sat down to warm his hands by the fire. As he leaned closer to the flames, he spied the stump on Pryvyd's right shoulder through the loose sleeve of his tunic. The skin where he had lost his arm was a pinkish brown and stretched extra tight over the remaining bone, much like Wily's own burn mark. *What could have possibly happened to Pryvyd?*

Wily suddenly realized that he was staring and quickly turned away. Then he felt self-conscious for turning away too fast. Pryvyd's eyes were on him.

"Did you scavenge for these mushrooms this morning?" Wily asked quickly, hoping to diffuse the situation with small talk.

"Plucked them right off Moshul's leg," Pryvyd said as he turned the spit. "He's like a walking salad. No need to ever get hungry when he's around."

As the knight shifted position, Wily noticed that the cloth shirt that clung to his chest bore the same strange symbol that decorated the shields of the Knights of the Golden Sun.

"Why do you have a golden octopus on your shirt?" Wily asked, curious.

Pryvyd looked down at himself and chuckled.

"That's how people here—the Panthasans—draw pictures of the sun," Pryvyd said.

Wily looked over at the sun that had only a short time earlier climbed above the distant mountain peaks. While it was impossible to look directly at it, there was one thing Wily was certain of: it did not have eight golden arms reaching out from it.

"But the sun is just a circle," Wily replied.

"It's a symbol meant to represent not just the sun, but the light that it casts upon the land," Pryvyd said, pulling his shirt tight. "And the group of knights I was once a part of believed that just like sunlight, kindness could warm all the land if given the chance to shine."

"That's a nice thought," Wily said.

"And a bunch of twiddle dump," Pryvyd continued. "I've been through enough to know."

Righteous, who was circling past them, gave Pryvyd a sharp elbow to the side of the head.

"I'm allowed to think whatever I want," Pryvyd called out to the arm as it floated along its patrol route. "You can go ahead and judge me."

Pryvyd pulled the skewer from the fire and examined the slightly charred mushrooms.

"They look ready," Pryvyd said as he offered one to Wily.

"I hope you've made plenty for everyone," Odette said, bounding over.

The elf cartwheeled into a full split, landing right beside Wily. With her bare hand, she grabbed a hot mushroom off the spit and popped it into her mouth.

"You must have gotten a good night's rest," Wily said.

"She's a morning elf," Pryvyd commented. "Which is a bit annoying if you ask me."

"The first hours of day have the most promise," Odette said. "It's when anything is possible."

"It's also when people should speak more quietly," Pryvyd replied. "Your enthusiasm is hurting my ears."

"Morning, Wily."

Roveeka came up behind the others, moving slower than usual. Wily could tell she had not slept well either. Her normally droopy eye was practically shut.

"It was hard to fall asleep last night," Roveeka said.

"Was it too bright for you as well?" Wily asked.

"Not at all," Roveeka replied. "I was just too busy examining these."

Roveeka held open her hand to reveal a dozen identical-looking pebbles.

Pryvyd slid another dozen mushrooms onto the skewer.

"We've been so busy running away," Wily said, "you never told me where we are going."

"Squalor Keep is first on our list," Odette said through bites. "A really nasty dungeon that's a day-and-a-half ride from here. The traps are rumored to be so tough that no one's been able to get past the first chamber."

"Which is why we've got you," Pryvyd added.

"If the legend is true," Odette gleamed, "great treasure stolen from the royal fortress is waiting in the final room of the keep. A dozen big raids like that and we'll have enough to pay our way to the Salt Isles on the finest ship."

"What's so great about the Salt Isles?" Roveeka asked.

"Not very much from what I hear," Odette answered. "It's a desolate place with jungles overrun by savage beasts. But there is one thing that makes it worth the trip. The air is so full of brine that it rusts metal within minutes. None of the Infernal King's machines work there."

"Why would you want to get away from the Infernal King?" Wily asked curiously.

The group stared at him. Wily shifted uncomfortably under their silence. Finally Pryvyd said, "He's an awful tyrant hated by all. He imprisons the innocent and destroys all that he cannot control."

Wily should have guessed this. Stalag had stuffed his head with a thousand lies about the Above. The sun didn't melt skin. Squirrels were not actually disguised evil magicians. He hadn't seen a single skullsucker eating a person's brains (if there was such a thing as a skullsucker at all). And the Infernal King was not the kind and generous ruler that Stalag had described.

Wily had many questions about the Infernal King.

"Why does the Infernal King do such terrible—"

"No," Odette snapped. "We're not talking about him. Not on such a beautiful morning."

"But I was just curious—"

"I said no," Odette cut him off again. "Save your questions about him for a rainy afternoon in a swamp. Enjoy the scent of the dawn blossoms."

With a hop and a skip, Odette bounded back to her sleeping blanket. In one quick movement, she folded it up and shoved it into her satchel.

"What's everyone waiting for?" Odette said impatiently. "If we move swiftly, we should be able to get to Squalor Keep before sundown tomorrow."

"Thankfully, she only stays this perky till noon," Pryvyd said under his breath to Wily and Roveeka. "Now, who wants seconds?"

AFTER A FEW hours travel, the group came upon a stone structure that fascinated Wily. It had four walls with a door and open holes at about shoulder height that could be used for looking in and out. The structure appeared positively inviting, not spooky or scary at all. He wondered if their trapsmith had grown ill or if they were just neglecting their duties.

As the group continued farther down the path, they began passing more of the small aboveground dungeons. Pryvyd told him they were actually called "houses."

The dirt path became cobblestone and the houses

began to appear closer and closer together. Yet there was not a person in sight.

"Where is everyone?" Pryvyd asked with a tinge of concern.

Ahead, a wooden sign was suspended from two poles on either side of the road.

"The Vale Village Willow Festival begins today," Odette said, eyeing the carved letters in the sign. "They must all be in the square."

"Is that what the sign says?" Wily asked, amazed. "You can read?"

"You can't?" Odette asked.

"Not a word."

"I would ask what cave you've been living in, but I already know the answer to that."

"Oh, for spike's sake," Wily said, suddenly aggravated. "I knew I should have grabbed all my books."

Then he remembered the gwarf's journal in his bag and a big smile burst across his face.

"I've got one! You can read it to me!"

"I don't do bedtime stories," she said with a shake of her head. "Ask Pryvyd."

Wily turned to the knight in awe.

"You can read, too?"

As they came over the rise, Wily could see all of Vale

Village, a maze of buildings with orange- and black-shingled rooftops nestled into a narrow valley. Pink and pale yellow banners embroidered with drooping trees stretched across the streets. In the center square, hundreds of people were gathered, dancing in circles and shouting happily.

"I certainly could use a drink," Pryvyd said with a smile. "And we need to pass through anyway."

"Fine," Odette said with a sigh, "but we're not sticking around for the puppet show."

As the group proceeded into the heart of Vale Village, Wily's eyes darted about, taking in this strange new place. Peeking through a window, Wily was amazed that there was an entire house that seemed to have shelves filled with only cooking utensils.

"How many spoons can one person possibly use?" Wily asked as they moved along to the next building. "Even if you were the greatest chef, you'd probably only need a few."

"It's a store," Pryvyd explained. "People come here to buy spoons."

"Buy?" Wily was unfamiliar with the concept.

"Yeah," Odette said. "What do you think gold coins are for?"

"Hoarding. Decorating your crypt. Letting them run through your fingers when you are coming up with an evil plan."

Odette rolled her eyes. Wily could tell she had a different answer to her question.

They passed a few more stores. One was filled with shields. Another with farming equipment. But Wily nearly tripped over himself when he looked inside the last building on the block.

Inside there were thousands of books of all shapes and sizes. Some were wrapped in leather, others were bound together with thin strips of parchment or metal clamps. He had never seen anything so wonderful in his life. (Except maybe the sunset. That was fairly impressive, too.)

"Look at them all," Wily said with his mouth agape.

He was at once lost in a dream of what these new books could tell him . . . imagining himself sitting under a tree's long arms, flipping pages as the tall ground moss tickled his toes.

"I know what you're going to be spending your gold on," Pryvyd said with a smile.

When they reached the edge of the square, they tied the two horses to a post and moved into the crowd.

Wily had never realized that there were so many people—humans, elves, gwarfs, or squatlings—in the whole world, let alone so many in a single town. They were all dressed in tunics and skirts colored the same pink and pale yellow as the banners hanging overhead. Everyone wore crowns and necklaces of wispy green leaves. Even more amazing was the fact that they were all smiling and laughing. He looked around trying to figure out what they were so happy about.

"Did they just find lost treasure or catch an enemy in a trap?" Wily asked Pryvyd as a circle of dancers swept past them.

"No," Pryvyd said. "They're celebrating the flowering of the willow tree. And the joy of being alive in this beautiful world."

Wily found this to be a strange but pleasant idea. Life was a constant slog in Carrion Tomb. *Is it possible that here in Panthasos happiness isn't as rare as finding a pearl in the mouth of a cave oyster?* He suddenly felt very bad for all the invaders he had helped trap in the mine below Carrion Tomb. He had believed their lives would be better working underground. But glancing around, he was quite certain that he had been wrong.

"Look, Wily," Roveeka said, pointing into the crowd. "It's a hobgoblet that looks just like you."

Following his half sister's line of sight, Wily spied a figure that did bear a modest resemblance to him. He was the same height and build. He held his back straight and had a row of tiny white teeth. He was sharing a bag of puffy yellow food with an older man and woman who greatly resembled him. Parents.

"Introduce yourself," Roveeka said to Wily, excited. "Maybe you're related."

"That's a human boy," Odette said.

Roveeka shook her head like that couldn't be possible. She moved through the crowd and tugged on the stranger's sleeve.

"I was wondering what breed of hobgoblet you are."

The boy let out a chuckle.

"I think you must be mistaken. I'm not a hobgoblet. . . ."

Wily knew what he was going to say even before the words came out of his mouth.

"I'm a human."

A huge lump formed in Wily's chest. It felt like he had just swallowed a boulder.

Roveeka furrowed her brow in confusion, but Wily felt like he had finally found clarity. This was the final piece of evidence. A truth that Wily could no longer ignore. He had always dreamed that there were hobgoblets just like him out here beyond the entrance of Carrion Tomb. He had just never thought that those hobgoblets were actually humans. Wily looked all around him. These were his kind. He had been lied to his entire life. He was torn between joy and loss. The heaviness in his chest eased slightly, and Wily had the strange sensation that his feet might lift off the ground.

"Are you okay?" Roveeka asked.

Wily was too busy pondering to answer. He couldn't trust anything Stalag had told him. *If my parents are human, are they* alive? *Are they out here somewhere in the Above? Was I kidnapped or did they give me away? Are they looking for me? Or do they know where I was taken?* The thoughts kept circling like eels trapped in a puddle. Or like the dancers spinning about him.

CLANG. CHUG. BANG.

Loud metallic sounds rang out in the distance.

Every person in the town square froze. The musicians stopped playing their instruments. A hand shot into the air and pointed to the hills.

"SNAGGLECARTS!" a woman screamed.

Four black beasts, each as large as a giant slug, rumbled down the streets of the village with their giant mouths agape. As Wily continued to stare in horror, he realized the black beasts weren't living creatures, but mechanical constructs made of cast iron.

All the villagers began running in terror. The Willow Festival had come to a horrible end.

"This," Odette said, "is the reason that we need to leave Panthasos and never return."

"What are they?" Roveeka asked.

Wily could now see that the metal beasts' mouths were like giant snap traps. He watched as one swallowed up a pair of fleeing villagers and thrust them into its caged belly. Through the bars, Wily could see people weeping and comforting their loved ones. The snaggle-cart was a trap on wheels.

"The Infernal King uses them to catch people and bring them . . . there . . ."

Pryvyd gestured to the mountain overlooking the village. Only it wasn't a mountain at all. Just the size of one.

"The prisonaut," Pryvyd continued.

The "mountain" was a slick metal structure on wheels with guard towers and walls a hundred feet tall. Spikes jutting from the sides of it rose and fell with every turn of the wheel. Armored figures patrolled the tops of the walls with crossbows.

Wily watched as a snagglecart filled with wailing villagers rolled up the prisonaut's extended ramp and through its open iron gate.

"Once you go in," Odette said grimly, "you never come out. We must leave here quickly!"

Wily felt a shiver go down his spine. Perhaps Carrion Tomb wasn't so bad after all.

9

SNAGGLECARTS AND GEARFOLK

"We need to get there," Odette said as she pointed to a hill on the far side of Vale Village.

Moshul chimed in with a few hand gestures as screaming villagers fled in every direction.

"Moshul's right," Pryvyd agreed. "If we try to double back and circumvent the town by crossing through the fields, we'll be easily spotted. There are spyglass spies on the roof of the prisonaut."

"And we'll risk walking right into Stalag and his scorpions," Odette said. "I say we try to creep through the town, using the buildings as cover. Blend in as best we can."

"I think both choices sound bad," Roveeka said.

Moshul nodded in agreement.

"We'll need to leave the horses behind," Pryvyd added. "They'll get easily spooked by the gearfolk and snagglecarts."

"Let's move before the gearfolk arrive," Odette said.

Wily and the others left the chaos of the main roads and began their stealthy journey through the back alleys of the town. Odette, creeping quickly from building to alcove, encouraged Wily, Roveeka, and Pryvyd to keep low and out of sight. Moshul tried his best to blend in as well. All the flowers sprouting from his body suddenly closed their buds. The green moss darkened into a deep gray. Even the mushrooms on his back sank deeper into the moist earth so their colorful crests weren't showing. Of course, he still looked like a giant walking pile of dirt.

Odette led the group down a twisting street of empty homes.

"Why would the Infernal King do this?" Wily asked.

"He's done far worse," Odette said. "Whole forests have been burned to the ground because the animals within them did not follow his commands. His only love is the machines that never question him."

"I think he would get along very well with Stalag," Roveeka said.

"Once we get to the Salt Isles," Pryvyd said, "neither the Infernal King nor Stalag will ever find us or you. We can finally live in peace. That's why it's so very important to collect enough treasure for passage on a sailing ship as soon as possible."

Up ahead, coming from the next crossroad, Wily could hear a sound he knew all too well. It was the sound of feet fleeing from danger, a frantic toe-heel, heel-toe clatter that sped up with every burst of panic.

A human woman clutching the hands of two barefoot girls came sprinting down the street, her eyes wide with fear.

"Faster!" the mother urged her children as she glanced over her shoulder. "And don't look back!"

Behind the fleeing trio, four metallic contraptions were rolling swiftly after them. Each resembled an equipment cart with a suit of armor and helmet attached to the front. Held in their metallic hands were long poles with hooks at the ends that resembled troll antlers. These must be the gearfolk.

"They look scared," Roveeka said. "We need to help them."

"You weren't concerned about helping people back in the tomb," Odette countered. "You let them get sent to the mines without a second thought."

Wily felt the sting of her words. She was right. He felt terrible about what he had done for all those years.

"But those were invaders," Roveeka explained, "not children."

"Do you want to get ourselves caught by the gear-folk, too?" Odette said. "There's nothing we can do."

Odette motioned the group to follow her into a narrow alcove between two buildings. Although now hidden, Wily still had a view of the street.

The fastest of the rolling gearfolk was now only five feet behind the mother and her two children. It swung the large pole through the air. The curved hook caught the ankle of the younger girl, tripping her. The girl's tiny hand was wrenched free from her mother's grasp as she fell to the cobblestoned ground.

"Keep going!" the mother said urgently to her older daughter as she broke hands with her. The mother doubled back for her fallen girl, who was now being seized by two gearfolk.

"We have to do something," Roveeka said as she pulled out Mum and Pops.

Wily nodded. He felt a deep tug in his heart, despite having never met these humans before. He wondered if his own mother had once tried to save him, too. Pryvyd looked pained by the situation, but he just shook his head.

"Mum and Pops could knock out two of them," Roveeka said, a determined look in her droopy eye. "And Moshul and you could take out the other two."

"And it would call the attention of a hundred more," Odette said, grabbing Roveeka by the wrist.

Just then, Righteous pulled its sword from Pryvyd's sheath. It left Pryvyd's side and started to fly in the direction of the mother and the fallen daughter.

"Get back here before I break off every one of your fingers," Pryvyd scolded.

"Don't you dare," Odette yelled after Righteous.

Odette made a running jump, flipping once in the air, before grabbing the wrist of the hovering arm. As soon as her feet hit the ground, she tried to tug it back toward the group's hiding spot, but Righteous was not going to give up without a fight. Righteous strained against Odette with all its might, dragging her feet along the bumpy street.

"A little help," Odette called back to the group.

Moshul reached out and grabbed Odette and Righteous in his mighty earthen hand.

Wily peeked from their hiding spot to see the eldest

daughter was running for a small hole in a stone wall. It was big enough for her to sneak through, but too tight a squeeze for the gearfolk on her tail. The girl was so close, only a few strides away—

A canister shot out from the gearfolk's midsection and opened midair, unleashing a net with weighted balls on each corner. It landed on the girl, entrapping her instantly.

She fell down hard but didn't give up. She was still crawling for the hole to escape.

Wily moved to help, but Pryvyd held him in place.

"It's the prisonaut for you!" shouted a shrill, high-pitched voice that came from the gearfolk's helmet.

"You can make it, Penpen!" the mother shouted to her eldest daughter as her own wrists were shackled together by a gearfolk.

Using only her elbows, the eldest daughter pulled herself along the ground to the hole in the wall. Then she disappeared inside it. The gearfolk had reached the hole a moment too late.

Thank all that is dark and scary, Wily thought to himself.

Undeterred, the gearfolk took its long hooked stick and shoved it inside the gap in the wall. Suddenly, the gearfolk let out a loud cackle. It pulled the stick from the hole, and there on the end was the girl, struggling and writhing.

Wily felt his heart sink.

"It'll be okay," the mother shouted, although to Wily it didn't sound like she really believed it.

"What did I say?" the gearfolk said with a laugh. "It's the prisonaut for you!"

Righteous struggled inside Moshul's large hand, trying to get free. Pryvyd looked like he was struggling as well. With himself.

"It's too late now," Odette said, pointing up the road.

One of the dragon-size snagglecarts was rolling toward the mother and children with its mechanical mouth open, hungry for more prisoners. Despite their terrible purpose, Wily couldn't help but admire the incredible skill with which they were built. The gearfolk, snagglecarts, and prisonaut were feats of engineering that rivaled his own creations. Even as the thought crossed his mind, he was ashamed of himself.

Through the metal bars of the machine's belly, Wily could see the faces of dozens of Panthasans, both young and old, all wearing expressions of hopelessness. *Did my traps in Carrion Tomb make the invaders feel this way?* He certainly hoped not.

The gearfolk prodded the mother and two daughters,

forcing them to walk up the ramp and into the jaws of the snagglecart.

"We'll just wait here until the cart passes," Odette said, stepping back into the alcove between the two buildings.

Moshul shook his head no.

"You're not going soft on me, too, are you?" Odette said. "I need a moss golem right now. Not a mud golem."

Moshul began signing with one hand as Righteous struggled to break free in the other.

"I don't know what you're trying to say," Odette said. "We can't wait here because . . . tomato sandwich? What are you saying?"

Clearly, the golem was used to signing with two hands. Moshul slouched, frustrated. Then he spun around and pointed back down the street from which they had come. After a moment, a trio of new gearfolk came into view.

Wily knew at once this was bad. They were trapped with nowhere to go. Unlike the tomb, there was no secret maintenance tunnel to hide in.

"It looks like this is a battle we're not going to be able to avoid," Pryvyd said.

The whole group huddled up together in the small crevice between two of the buildings. They needed to keep the element of surprise for as long as they could. They would be spotted in a moment when the gear-folk passed near, and they needed any advantage they could get.

Wily scanned his surroundings for a path of escape, but he wasn't finding anything. Until, out of the corner of his eye, he spotted something on a rooftop across the street. It was a figure. A person wrapped in a cloak and an assortment of yellow, blue, and green scarves.

Before he could get a longer look, the figure darted out of view. A moment later, he spied what looked to be a pair of long, skinny rats shimmying down a drainpipe. The rats leaped from the stone wall of the building to a tree. A second leap took them to the snagglecart, and they disappeared inside it.

"Stay close together," Pryvyd said, dragging Wily's attention back to the situation at hand and holding his spiked shield in front of him. "I won't be able to defend you if you're not next to me."

The trio of gearfolk was almost upon them. Roveeka pulled out Mum and Pops as Moshul loosened his grip on Righteous. Wily steeled himself for the inevitable encounter.

Just then, a loud grinding sound came from the snagglecart. Wily looked out to see smoke pouring from the gears of the black beast. The jaws of the great machine were struggling to close and it was clear something was preventing them from doing so.

Inside the belly of the beast, the prisoners all dropped to their knees and covered their heads.

BOOM!

The front of the snagglecart exploded into a twisted mess of metal. The barred gate that kept the prisoners from escaping blew wide open. All the captured humans fled toward the nearby woods as it started to break into more pieces under the stress of its own dislodged gears.

"Don't let them escape!" a gearfolk shouted in a high-pitched shriek.

Two of the mechanical soldiers turned to speed after the fleeing humans. Yet as soon as they began to move, their wheels popped free of their undercarriage and rolled into the gutter.

Wily couldn't understand how this was happening. Then he saw a rodent squirm out of one the gearfolk's inner workings. It tossed a dozen screws on the ground as it leaped inside a new gearfolk. *The rodent disabled the gearfolk.*

The trio of gearfolk that Pryvyd and Odette were preparing to face in battle instead ran straight past

Wily and the others. They had more pressing matters to attend to now.

"This is our opportunity," Odette said aloud. "Let's move."

The entire group took off, sprinting past the malfunctioning snagglecart as sprockets and gears erupted in every direction like bubbles of magma from a belching lava beast.

As Wily sprinted, he spied the mother and her two daughters, again hand in hand, running down an alley. But they weren't free yet. The gearfolk that had pulled the eldest daughter from the hole in the wall was in quick pursuit.

"I can't keep up," the youngest daughter cried out. Her large brown eyes swam with tears as her small legs quivered. "I'm tired."

Wily slowed. He had to help.

"Don't even think about it," Odette said, grabbing his wrist.

Wily saw the gearfolk reach out his hooked stick for the little girl's ankle.

Before it was able to snare her, though, the cloaked figure from the rooftop dropped from above. The figure landed on the gearfolk's back and grabbed the steel helmet of the machine. With a quick turn to the left, a twist to the right and a double-pump down, the helmet popped off the gearfolk, leaving it headless.

The eldest daughter looked back in awe.

"The Scarf!" she exclaimed.

The scarf-covered figure then reached into the open neck of the mechanical man and pulled out a small cage. Inside was a small figure that looked like a miniature hobgoblin with rust-colored wings. Its four arms were each holding a tiny mechanical lever.

"Put me back!" the small creature screeched loudly as the mother and two children disappeared down the cluttered alley. Wily sighed with relief. They were finally safe.

The cloaked figure—what did the girl call it? The Scarf?—opened the cage and threw the flying creature into the air. It flitted away in disgust.

Wily wanted to stay and watch what the Scarf did next, but Odette was pulling him toward the far side of town.

"There are many more gearfolk and snagglecarts," Odette said, "and the Scarf won't be able to save us from all of them—"

The words had barely left her mouth when Wily turned to see a pair of gearfolk rolling swiftly toward him. Their hooked sticks were pointed at his chest like spears. Wily fumbled with his tool belt, desperately looking for something to stop them.

Fortunately, Odette was not so slow.

She rushed past him and scooped up two fallen snagglecart gears. Gripping them in her palms with the teeth poking out between her fingers, she somersaulted over the first gearfolk's hooked sticks and landed in between its metal arms. With a swift and powerful punch to the chest, she knocked him backward off his wheels. Then, with lightning reflexes, she struck the other gearfolk with an uppercut hit that sent his head spinning.

"Just be glad she's on our side," Pryvyd said to an awed Wily. "I can't tell you how many times she's saved my neck."

As Wily and his companions winded their way out of town, he was able to get one final look at the giant prisonaut rolling its way into the village. There, in one of the high towers, Wily saw an ominous figure wearing a bloodred helmet with three mighty horns sticking out from it. The figure loomed over the spiked walls of the steel juggernaut, watching his gearfolk work.

A bitter chill crawled over Wily's skin. He had seen the Infernal King for the first time, and he could only hope that it would be his last.

10

A MISPLACED MAP

"The Scarf is a mysterious figure," Pryvyd explained as he led the group along the narrow path at the base of the canyon. "Some say she is an elf princess. Others claim that he is a wizard. Still others say that there is no one beneath the scarves at all and that it is just a ghost of a hero from long ago."

Wily's eyes drifted to the high cliffs on either side of the path. Pryvyd had said this place was called Drayback Canyon. It reminded him of the crushing walls of Carrion Tomb's Hall of Axes. Although they were not actually moving slowly toward one another with grim certainty, they appeared to get closer together the farther the group progressed. It hardly seemed scary compared to what they had just survived, though.

When Wily and his companions had made it to the woods on the far side of Vale Village, they had hidden among the blossoming willow trees. Fortunately, the forest had been too dense for the snagglecarts and the willow roots too bumpy for the small-wheeled gearfolk to traverse. Wily and his companions had waited there silently for a long stretch before continuing on their journey. Now, many hours later, they were traveling across the very different landscape of Drayback Canyon.

"In fact," Odette added, "all that is known about the Scarf is that she or he works alone, destroying the contraptions of the Infernal King."

"Not completely alone," Wily said, snapping back to the conversation. "Did you see those skinny rats helping?"

"Can't say that I did," Pryvyd answered.

"It was the rats who broke the snagglecart," Wily added, "and pulled off the wheels of the gearfolk."

The others shook their heads. Even though no one else was able to confirm Wily's claim, he was quite sure of what he had seen.

As they proceeded farther into the canyon, Wily

was treated to a magnificent sight. Stone statues of giants lined the high cliff walls like columns. They were enormous, five times taller than Moshul. Each was carved with incredible detail, every muscle and wrinkle articulated with perfect precision. Their white eyes appeared to be made of polished crystalline quartz. The statues were so lifelike Wily could almost imagine them breathing.

Then one turned his head and looked directly at them.

Wily nearly jumped back into Pryvyd's arm.

"They're alive?" Wily wondered aloud.

"As alive as Moshul," Odette responded. "They're golems as well. Stone golems."

"Will they attack us?" Roveeka asked nervously.

"Not without someone to command them," Odette continued. "Their masters have long ago disappeared. Now they just stand here waiting for them to return. A golem always needs a master."

"Even Moshul?" Roveeka asked, patting the tangle of vines on the moss golem's head.

"Moshul was a mistake," Odette said. "In fact, the wizard that made him was trying to create another great stone golem just like the ones standing here. But something went wrong with the spell. Instead of the tough rocks from the ground forming a great warrior, only the soft moist earth rose up. Once the wizard realized his mistake, he didn't even bother to finish the conjuring spell. That's why Moshul has no mouth."

Wily looked at Moshul and suddenly saw the moss golem in a very different light. Before, he had seemed large, imposing, and confident, but now he seemed small and a bit sad, like the toothless runt in a litter of gristle hounds.

"The wizard left him alone in the woods with no goal or purpose," Odette continued. "And Moshul just sat there. Waiting. For years, he just sat. When I found him, he was still sitting in the same spot in which he had been left. A whole garden had grown on his back. Knowing that his own master would never return, I offered to have him join me. For him to be his own master."

Wily suddenly felt as if he had more in common with the moss golem than anybody else in the whole world. For years, Wily would throw stones into the lava pools of Carrion Tomb, hoping that they would grant his wish for a true family. But those wishes, like the stones themselves, had just melted away.

"From now on," Roveeka said to the golem from atop his shoulders, "you're going to be getting a lot of extra hugs."

The hobgoblet wrapped her arms tightly around Moshul's neck and squeezed. Wily couldn't be sure, but he thought that the moss golem appreciated it.

At the end of the row of statues, the group passed beneath a stone archway formed by the extended arms of the final two golems. Just beyond it, the canyon walls dropped away, revealing a vista of rocky hills. Their single path ended, branching into dozens of possible directions in which to head.

Odette came to a stop and untied the drawstrings of her everstuff satchel. She reached inside and began to jangle around, looking for something.

"I know I put the map in here somewhere," Odette said.

"I'm not sure how you can find anything inside that bag," Pryvyd said with a sigh. "I told you to keep it in your pocket instead."

"Got it!"

Excitedly, she pulled a rolled piece of parchment out of the bag. She tore the cloth twist tie off and unfurled it. As soon as she saw what was written on it, she deflated.

"Wrong map," Odette said. "This is the one for the hidden treasure of Brine Crater."

She rolled it up and shoved it back inside.

"It was right near the top by the spare lanterns,"

Odette said with mild aggravation. "At least until Moshul started shoving the treasure from Carrion Tomb's vault inside."

Moshul narrowed his eyes and began signing to Odette.

"I know we were in a rush," Odette responded to moss golem, "but you could have at least made sure not to knock over everything. You even tipped one of the bookshelves."

Wily was getting very confused.

"I'm sorry . . . but how exactly does that bag work?"

"It's an everstuff satchel," Odette clarified. "Come over here and take a look."

Wily approached Odette, who still had her arm, from fingertips to shoulder, shoved deep inside. He leaned over as she opened the mouth of the satchel wider.

Wily had realized that this was no ordinary bag, but he was hardly prepared for what he saw within. The inside was at least double the size of Stalag's vault, with full-size shelves and storage cases packed with bottles and boxes and books and weapons hugging the silk walls of the bag. Messily dumped on its curved floor was the pile of treasure stolen from Carrion Tomb. Wily realized that if he had one of these bags, he could keep every book in the whole world inside.

"That's amazing," Wily said, "but how can you reach the stuff at the very bottom?"

"Pick something and give it try," Odette replied.

Wily looked into the everstuff satchel and spied a bottle of clear liquid on a far shelf. He reached in to grab it, and as he did, he felt his arm stretch. The bones and muscles in his arm became malleable, like the gooey body of an amoebolith. His fingers wrapped around the glass vial and gave it a tug. As he pulled out his arm, his bones and muscles returned to normal and the glass vial in his hand was perfectly intact.

"You don't want to reach too far inside, though," Pryvyd said. "If you fall in, you'd need someone else to pull you out."

Odette took the bottle from Wily and stuck it back into the bag. She started rummaging around inside again.

"The map had gold leaf with a silver tie," Odette said in huff. "I'm sure of it."

"You mean, like this one?" Roveeka asked.

The group all turned to look at her. There in her hand was a rolled scroll with a silver tie.

"It was sticking out of your back pocket," Roveeka said with a self-satisfied smile.

"Which you probably put there so you wouldn't lose it," Pryvyd said.

Odette didn't bother to respond. She grabbed the map out of Roveeka's hand and unrolled it. Wily glanced down at it as well.

He wasn't able to read words, but he had no problem with maps. They were often helpful in Carrion Tomb for showing the hobgoblets where to stand to perform the perfect ambush or for reminding Roveeka how to get from the dining room to the Chamber of Shield and Helm in the shortest amount of time. Wily would even draw his own maps of the tomb and leave them lying about. He remembered watching unwitting invaders snatch them up, thinking they had found a shortcut to the vault only to discover that the map was completely incorrect and that they had been tricked into walking in circles.

"This is the entrance to Squalor Keep," Odette said as she pointed to a spot marked on the map with a doorway, "and we're over here." She pointed to another spot farther north on the map. "So we should be going that way."

Odette stretched her arm to the hills beyond a field of prickly bushes.

"Actually, I think we might be here," Wily said, pointing to a very different spot on the map, east of the other. "It looks like this is the canyon we just exited. Which means we should head in that direction."

Wily pointed off toward a different set of hills with sharp rocks jutting out of them.

"I think Wily may be right," Pryvyd said as he took a glance at the map.

Odette twisted the map slightly, and then quickly answered. "Yes, that's what I meant."

Before even rolling up the map, Odette began marching toward the hills with the sharp rocks.

Wily felt a nudge on his side. He turned to see that it was Pryvyd giving him a gentle elbow. The bald knight nodded silently as if to say, *Well done.*

IT TOOK ALL day and a few hours into the next day to reach the hill with the jutting rocks that, according to the map, housed the entrance to Squalor Keep. Once they arrived, however, they discovered that finding the door was going to be more difficult than they had thought. There was no clearly labeled sign or spookily decorated path to show the way. It was just a maze of angular rocks, identical snake mounds, and tufts of wild grass. After an hour of fruitless searching, even Odette was beginning to lose her patience.

"There must be a spell of some kind hiding the

entrance of the keep," Odette surmised. "It's the only explanation."

Wily was quite familiar with illusions of this sort. Stalag used one to hide the rolling boulder in the Temple of Foreboding. Others he cast to disguise the maintenance tunnel doors behind layers of dripping mold. Stalag had even once tried to create an illusion to make it seem like there was a stone floor where the acid pool sat. It looked perfect, but illusions were unable to hide smells, and the toxic fumes were a pungent clue that something wasn't quite right.

"It's here somewhere," Pryvyd said as he pressed his attached hand up against a jagged rock. "One of these rocks must be enchanted. Start pushing."

Moshul gave a nearby boulder a shove, knocking it over. It nearly crushed Roveeka, who stumbled out of the way just in time to avoid becoming squashed hobgoblet.

"Gently, Moshul," Pryvyd added.

Moshul started signing to Roveeka. Wily could tell by his posture and mortified expression that he was trying to apologize.

"That's okay," Roveeka said kindly back to him. "It was an accident. I have them all the time."

For the next hour, Wily felt like he had pushed on

a thousand stones. Even his callused hands that were accustomed to manual labor were starting to feel tired. He sat down for a brief rest.

As the night sky filled with stars, Wily was surprised to feel a wave of homesickness wash over him. Being out in the Above was beyond his expectations, especially since his skin hadn't melted off. Yet, in this moment, he missed the spiders and the slugs, the quiet solitude of his sleeping chamber, and the dank musty odor that drifted slowly through the twisting corridors deep below the ground.

He could almost smell it now. The scent of cobwebs and mold spore drifting through the air was remarkably vivid.

Then Wily realized that the scent was not a memory or his imagination. He could smell it right now. He breathed in deeply. There was a dungeon nearby.

"We're close," Wily shouted. "Very close."

Wily leaped to his feet and started following his nose. Taking steps to the left and then to the right like a gristle hound sniffing a scrap of meat dropped on the floor. The scent grew stronger as he moved to a patch of tall dry grass on the side of a hill. *Could this be it?*

He stuck his hands out to touch the hillside and his

fingers went right through it, along with the rest of his body.

"Wily?" Roveeka called out. "Where'd you go?"

"Over here," he yelled back in response.

Wily stuck his hand and head out of the illusionary hill. The others hurried over and stepped inside.

The entrance to Squalor Keep was a long rectangular hallway with perfectly smooth walls. Unlike Carrion Tomb, which was a series of natural caves with natural stalactites and lava pools, this dungeon appeared to have been constructed entirely by tools. Wily picked up some stone grains off the ground and ran them through his fingertips.

"This is newly carved stone," Wily said. "When was Squalor Keep built?"

"Stories of this dungeon began to spread a little over a decade ago, right before the reign of the Infernal King," Odette explained as they started down the dark hall. "They say a servant of the old king stole many great valuables from the castle's treasury and hid them here behind a hundred dangers, never to be found by man or elf again."

"Can hobgoblets find the treasure?" Roveeka asked. "They weren't mentioned in the story."

"I think they're included in the man or elf part," Odette said, rolling her eyes.

Roveeka seemed disappointed by this. Moshul lifted his palm, sending a cloud of fireflies ahead to illuminate their path.

"Lead the way, Wily," Pryvyd said.

"And remember," Odette added, "our lives are in your hands."

Wily swallowed hard. It was a lot of pressure on his small shoulders. His eyes darted in every direction as they made their way down the dimly lit tunnel.

The thick layer of dust on the floor meant either one of two things: Squalor Keep had an excellent trapsmith that was incredibly skilled at making it seem creepy and desolate or the dungeon actually hadn't been explored in years.

A bit farther, Wily spotted a skeleton on the floor that was missing both of its legs.

"Very nice touch," Wily remarked. "I like the trail of chipped bones that make it look like he was desperately trying to escape. And those words scrawled into the dirt by his extended finger are inspired."

Odette looked down and read the words aloud.

TURN BACK NOW.

"Great detail," Wily said, then realizing that this might not be the work of a trapsmith: "Or dying words that we should be taking very seriously."

"Don't worry," Roveeka said. "Nothing bad will happen when you're leading the way."

This didn't make Wily feel any better. He scanned for falling spikes and trip wires as they proceeded deeper down the rectangular tunnel, eying decorations on the walls that were useful for hiding blowguns or swinging pendulum blades. But he didn't find anything out of the ordinary.

Ahead of them was a perfectly square room. It was also a dead end with three smooth walls and a floor that appeared to be made of one solid piece of stone.

"I can't see any drop pits or pressure plates," Wily said.

"Or doors," Pryvyd added.

"Could there be another illusion?" Odette asked.

"Two illusions in a row?" Wily scoffed. "That wouldn't be very creative, would it?"

"No one was trying to win an architectural award," Odette countered, "just trying to keep people away from the treasure."

"Trust me," Wily said. "You never go back-to-back with the same trick or trap."

"Maybe we missed something," Pryvyd said. "Should we turn around?"

Moshul nodded enthusiastically and Righteous gave a thumbs-up. The fireflies fluttered back the other way.

"Maybe the skeleton wasn't a warning, but a clue," Odette wondered.

Moshul, Righteous, and Pryvyd turned around and were the first to leave the square room. As soon as they crossed the threshold, there was a loud CLICK. Before anyone could do a thing, a stone wall dropped from the ceiling, blocking Wily, Odette, and Roveeka's way out.

11

EVERSTUFFED

"I can't see anything," Odette screamed.

Wily couldn't see anything either: without Moshul's fireflies, it had become pitch black. His eyes had been excellent at seeing in the dark, but after spending so much time in the Above, they were having problems adjusting. Roveeka's hobgoblet eyes must have been more adaptable.

"That's good," Roveeka said, "because I don't think you want to see this."

Wily felt a series of low rumbling vibrations. He knew that sensation very well. The walls were beginning to close in on them.

Crushing walls. How did I miss that? No wonder there are no cobwebs on the ceiling or bats hanging above.

SCHCKKK.

Wily heard what sounded like metal scratching against rock, and suddenly there was light. Odette now held a lit torch in one hand and the everstuff satchel in the other. The walls were already half the distance apart that they had been when the group had first entered the room.

"How do we stop them?" Odette said in a panic.

"There must be an emergency lever or button some-where," Wily said.

Odette and Roveeka scanned the rapidly tightening room.

"Don't see one," Roveeka said.

"Just keep calm," said Wily, who was growing ner-vous himself. "There's always a way out. You just need to know what to do."

The walls were getting closer now. If he stretched his arms out, they could nearly touch both of the walls at the same time.

"Maybe in Carrion Tomb," Odette said urgently, "but I don't think the person who built this keep fol-lowed the same guidelines."

Just then, the walls stopped moving.

"See?" Wily said with a relieved smile. "What did I tell you?"

And then the ceiling started to drop.

"We're going to be flattened!" Odette yelled. "I can't believe I trusted you."

Wily's mind was racing. She was right. They were going to be crushed. There was nowhere to go. Nowhere to hide.

Then Wily spied the answer.

He grabbed the everstuff satchel off Odette's shoulder.

"There's nothing in there that can stop these walls," Odette admonished.

"I know," Wily said. "We're not taking anything out. We're putting something in."

Wily opened the mouth of the bag wide.

"Us."

He turned to Roveeka.

"Jump inside."

She didn't hesitate. The hobgoblet dove headfirst into the bag.

"This is crazy," Odette said. "We can't—"

Odette was about to protest more when the dropping ceiling touched the top of her head. She leaped with both feet into the satchel.

Wily put the everstuff satchel on the floor and stepped through the mouth of the bag. As Wily disappeared inside, he heard the roof crush against the floor with a final thud.

With a clatter, Wily fell on a pile of jade goblets, only narrowly missing the sharp tip of a jewel-encrusted sword. Odette, of course, was standing nearby, having landed perfectly on her feet. Roveeka's head and torso were buried in a heaping pile of gold coins. She was kicking and making muffled cries.

Wily looked up and saw that the ceiling had indeed collapsed completely down upon the bag. Odette spun around to face him.

"I know what you're going to say," Wily said, prepared for Odette's anger. "'Now we're stuck in here.'"

"Took the words right out of my mouth," Odette said. Then, softening, she added, "But at least we're not crushed."

Wily couldn't help but smile.

"Should we give your sister a hand?" Odette said, eyeing the flailing hobgoblet.

"I think that would be a good idea."

Wily grabbed one of Roveeka's legs and Odette grabbed the other. With a heave, they pulled the hobgoblet free.

Roveeka gave her head a shake as she sat up.

"Grumpf-rumphed."

She moved her jaw to the left and then to the right . . . and spit out a gold coin.

Now that everyone was okay, Wily took a closer look at his surroundings. The satchel's curved walls reached impossibly high and tapered at the top and at the bottom. There was no easy way to climb to the hole above. Even if he stood on the tippy top of the bookcases affixed to the walls, he would still be many arm lengths below the exit of the everstuff satchel. There was some good news, though—through the bag's opening, Wily could see that the collapsing roof was rising again.

Odette tried running up one of the walls, but they were not stiff like a stone, but rather flexible like a silk curtain. There was no way for her to gain traction.

"I can't get a good enough grip with my hands," Odette said.

"What if," Roveeka said, "you used a pair of sharp knives like Mum and Pops to climb the walls."

"We can't risk ripping the satchel," Odette said. "Even the slightest tear will destroy the magic and make all the belongings inside disappear."

"I don't want to disappear," Roveeka said, stating the obvious.

"Me neither," Odette agreed.

"We could make a grappling hook," Wily suggested as he dug in the pile of treasure. "With a jagged piece of crystal and this rope."

Odette lifted the two found objects in her hands to measure their weight. Then shook her head.

"The crystal is heavy," Odette announced, "but the rope is even heavier. We'll never be able to toss it all the way up and through the mouth of the bag."

Wily slumped, realizing she was right.

"I found something that might work," Roveeka said, holding up some very fine black twine. "If I tie it around Mum, I could throw it out the top of the bag."

Odette came over and examined the long coil of black thread. She gave it a taut pull and then yanked on it even harder.

"It's like steel but as light as a pixie wing!" Odette said. "It must be enchanted thread."

She ran her finger over the stretch of fiber, examining it.

"What's strange is that I've never seen it before," Odette continued. "I thought I'd seen everything that Moshul had put in the bag."

"Maybe it fell out of one of Stalag's treasure chests,"

Wily guessed. "He'd hoarded so much that even he didn't know what he had in that vault."

"I guess it doesn't matter where it came from," Odette added. "It's a way out."

Roveeka knotted the end of the shimmering black thread to the hilt of Mum.

"Make sure you get it straight out of the hole," Odette slowly and clearly explained. "Even the smallest puncture hole in the fabric could have disastrous effects."

"My sister never misses," Wily said confidently, choosing to ignore his slight doubts.

Odette braced herself as Roveeka pulled the knife back behind her head.

"Up you go, Mum," Roveeka whispered to herself.

Then the hobgoblet let her knife fly.

Mum soared through the air, tumbling tip over hilt with the enchanted thread trailing behind it. Wily looked ahead to try to anticipate the blade's trajectory. It looked like it was going to hit the side of the satchel. He held his breath with dread.

But he should have never doubted Roveeka's skills; the knife flew directly out of the bag.

"Yes!" Wily said as the serrated edge of the knife embedded itself in the stone wall above.

As it did, Wily heard a loud—RIP.

"What was that?" Odette said.

"I didn't hit the satchel," Roveeka said, confused.

Beneath their feet, the ground was beginning to give way. Gold coins were being sucked out from under their feet, like they were being swallowed up by a pool of quicksand.

Odette saw that the black thread was taut. She followed the twine down to its now visible origin. It wasn't an enchanted rope from Stalag's dungeon. It was the magical thread that held together the seam of the everstuff satchel. And now that seam was opening up.

"Start climbing!" Odette shouted as she grabbed her puzzle box from a nearby shelf and leaped onto the thread.

The acrobatic elf started to scamper to the top with incredible speed. Roveeka tried to follow after her but was not nearly as fast. Wily was stuck taking up the tail.

As he climbed, he looked below to see that the hole in the everstuff satchel was getting bigger and bigger. Coins and chests and magical swords dropped through the ever-expanding opening and into a black void darker and more terrifying than the depths of Carrion Tomb's bottomless pit.

"Faster!" Odette screamed back to the others as she pulled herself out of the mouth of the satchel.

Just above Wily, Roveeka was slowing down.

"My arms," Roveeka wheezed. "I can't."

Wily glanced down again as the bookshelves were torn from the walls and tumbled into the darkness. Even the very air around Wily was being sucked into the magical void.

Peering back inside the satchel, Odette could see that Roveeka wasn't going to make it on her own and began pulling the thread upward toward her. Roveeka and Wily were getting closer to the mouth of the bag, but each of Odette's yanks also ripped the seam of the satchel open faster, causing the little treasure left in the everstuff satchel to vanish.

Wily could feel his whole body being pulled and stretched as the satchel's magic began to dissipate. He put one hand over the next, trying to block out the swirling nothingness that was now surrounding him. There was no way he would be able to get out in time.

Then, to his surprise, he saw Odette reaching down into the bag. She grabbed Roveeka's hand.

"Hold on to Roveeka's leg!" Odette called out to Wily.

Wily reached up and grabbed hold of his sister's bulbous ankle.

He felt himself being pulled up and down at the

same time. He wasn't sure which direction he was going in. . . .

A moment later he found himself on the floor of the Chamber of Crushing Walls. The torn everstuff satchel lay ruined at his feet, everything that had been inside of it now gone. And if it hadn't been for Odette, he'd have disappeared, too. She had saved his and Roveeka's lives.

Wily felt Odette standing over him. He slowly raised his head to meet her gaze—and saw that she was furious.

"You know what that is?" Odette said, pointing to the everstuff satchel. "Eight months of plundering gone."

"At least we're safe," Roveeka said as she slid Mum back into her waistband.

"Says the hobgoblet who hasn't spent the better part of a year ransacking haunted castles and monster-filled temples," Odette fumed. "This is going to put us back months. I wanted to set sail for the Salt Isles before winter. Now we might miss that window if we don't get lucky with a really big find."

"It was an accident," Wily said defending Roveeka from Odette's poison-filled eyes.

"An accident that should have never happened." Odette turned her anger on Wily. "It was your job to spot the traps before we stepped into them. We never would have dared to enter here if we thought we had a dud trapsmith. I'm not sure why the Oracle of Oak thought that you, of all trapsmiths, were the one we should seek out."

"I think you should have let her get squashed," Roveeka said to Wily quietly.

"Do you want to live in a land where the Infernal King could snatch you up at any moment in a snagglecart?" Odette snapped back. "Because I don't. And our best chance out of Panthasos just went tumbling through a ripped seam."

The wall that had shut on Moshul and Pryvyd on the other end of the room was still closed, but Wily could now hear banging coming from the other side. Odette clearly heard it, too, as she went running to the stone wall.

"Is there a way to open it without setting off the trap again?" Odette wondered aloud.

Wily took a quick look around. A new hallway lit with glowing purple crystals had appeared where the dead end had been before. This was no surprise to Wily. Just like in Carrion Tomb, most dead ends were only dead ends for those who didn't know where the secret switch to the next passage was. Wily found a hidden lever tucked behind a stone pyramid. He gave it a sharp pull.

The wall slid back up into the ceiling, revealing their companions behind it.

"Thank the Golden Sun above that you're okay," Pryvyd said. "We feared the worst."

"It almost was," Odette said. "More than once."

Moshul hurried over to Odette and lifted her up into a giant hug.

"Easy now," Odette said. "I'm more breakable than you are."

The moss golem didn't seem to care. Even the vines dangling from his shoulders squeezed her tightly.

Pryvyd came up behind Odette and put a tender hand on her shoulder, while Righteous put his hand on her other one.

"I'm not letting you get out of my sight again," Pryvyd said.

"Even in the morning?" Odette asked.

"Especially in the morning," Pryvyd replied. "That's when you get into the most trouble."

Wily looked at the odd foursome: a one-armed knight, a hovering arm, a blue-haired elf, and a golem of moss and earth. When he had first spied them in the tomb, he thought they were as different as any four could be, but right now, they looked a lot like a family.

THE LORD OF
SQUALOR KEEP

The hallway of glowing crystals led the group into an imposing room with high vaulted ceilings. The painted black walls were adorned with swords and axes, some so huge only a giant could wield them, while others appeared to be made for the tiniest squatling. A stone sparring ring formed a circle in the center of the chamber.

On the opposite side of the room, sitting in a stone chair, was a creature that looked like it could have sprung from a night terror. From the waist up, it appeared to be a mighty human warrior with a thick beard and a thicker nest of twisted horns bursting from his skull, but in place of legs, it had a red-and-yellow-striped snake tail coiled on the floor.

The demonic creature was fast asleep and didn't look up when Wily and the others entered. In fact, he was so deep in slumber that he was mumbling to himself.

"Perhaps we can tiptoe around it," Odette whispered to the others.

Yet, before they could, the creature stirred. He looked up at them and then back down at the ground. Then, as though suddenly realizing what he had seen, the creature's head popped back up in surprise.

"Are you real?" the snake-tailed warrior coughed out, his voice dry as if he hadn't spoken in a long time.

"I think so," Roveeka said, looking down at her own arms.

"Excellent!" the creature said with excitement. "You must do battle with me—no—wait, I missed a part."

The snake creature was flustered. He tried again.

"Welcome to Squalor Keep." He looked unsure of himself. "It's not 'welcome'—it's—hold on a second—I want to get this right."

The snake warrior reached into his suit of emerald armor and fumbled around inside. He pulled out a piece of paper and quickly read it over.

"Those who dare enter Squalor Keep," the snake warrior intoned in a booming authoritative voice, "must face battle with me in the Ring of Blades!"

The warrior reached over and lifted a rusty sword covered in moss. It was not a scary sight. Just kind of sad and pathetic. The snake warrior looked defeated.

"My apologies. I've never done this before."

"Never?" Pryvyd asked.

The snake warrior shook his head.

"You're the only adventurers to get past the Crushing Room."

"Ever?" Odette asked.

The snake warrior nodded.

"The lord of the keep told me to wait here until the first intruders came and report back to him after they were defeated. So I've been waiting. And waiting."

"You haven't left this room?" Wily questioned.

"I'm a Summoned One," the demon snake said. "Following orders very specifically is what we do."

"That must have been . . . ," Roveeka said, ". . . boring."

"It hasn't been the best ten years of my eternal life. But I've found ways to keep busy. I made a mushroom garden for myself. I do a lot of counting in my head. Sometimes I make little dolls out of clumps of moss."

The Summoned One held up a small green doll with a snake tail.

"You're very talented," Roveeka said earnestly.

The Summoned One blushed.

"So," the Summoned One said reluctantly, "who should I fight to the death first?"

"I will do battle with you," Pryvyd said as he pulled out his sword.

"No," Odette said. "Let me."

"Or nobody has to fight," Wily said. "If you bring us to the lord of Squalor Keep. You can tell us more about, um, your life here along the way."

The Summoned One considered.

"But I was told very clearly—"

"We could always go back to fighting to the death," Wily reassured the Summoned One.

"And you promise not to hurt the master . . ."

"We will not lift a finger to harm him," Wily said.

"Then there shall be no battle today," the Summoned One said as he put down the sword. "This way."

The Summoned One slithered over to an axe on the wall and gave it a few cranks. A secret door to what looked like the maintenance passages slid open.

As the Summoned One led the group down a series of ramps and stone staircases, he told them in rich detail about his time in the keep. He was about to launch into a description of the fifth step in creating moss dolls when Wily interrupted to spare the group.

"I used to work in Carrion Tomb," he told the Summoned One. "I could explain to your lord that your working conditions here are really unfair. You should at least have regular breaks and a proper sleep chamber. Even the creatures of my old dungeon were given those basic rights."

"I would love for someone to speak on my behalf," the Summoned One said. "The master can be very kind, but also quite moody. I suppose it all stems back to his time before the keep."

"Really?" Wily said, preparing for another long explanation.

"Yes!" the Summoned One explained, clearly taking Wily's response as a sign of interest. "Before building Squalor Keep, the lord was the chief engineer for the royal family of Panthasos. He built many wonders of the land, including King Gromanov's castle, the Aqueducts of the Arid Plains, and the Great Mole Machine that tunneled beneath Cloudscrape Peak. The other part of his job, and his greatest passion, was teaching the king's children math and science.

"He took a particular interest in the youngest of the king's three children, Kestrel Gromanov. He was neither strong like his eldest brother nor inspiring like his middle sister, but he was incredibly skilled with machines.

My master taught him all his tricks and, in a short time, he was creating devices that had taken my master many years to learn how to construct. Kestrel wanted desperately to impress his father with his inventions, but the king still favored his older siblings. My master watched as Kestrel grew increasingly jealous as the years passed."

Wily was surprised to find his interest piqued.

"One day, my lord came down to the castle basement laboratory and found Kestrel working on a mechanical weapon too dangerous to be put out into the world. He confronted Kestrel and the two nearly came to blows. Kestrel apologized, but my lord sensed something very bad growing in him."

Wily noticed the Summoned One's voice lowered whenever he spoke about Kestrel. "That night while my lord lay in bed, a mechanical man tried to kill him in his sleep. It was clearly Kestrel's work. My lord managed to escape, but he realized that Kestrel had grown too powerful and would attempt to overthrow his father. So he decided to flee the castle with the Gromanov family's most valuable treasures to keep them safe until Kestrel was defeated."

"Kestrel is still in power," Odette told the Summoned One. "But now he's known by another name. The Infernal King."

Wily thought back to the frightening figure he had seen standing atop the prisonaut, wearing the bloodred helmet. An alarming thought went through his head. The cruel overlord of Panthasos had once been a boy fascinated by machines just like himself. He shivered.

The Summoned One stopped in his tracks, his snake tail curling around itself.

"The lord will be very upset to hear this," the Summoned One said, his voice dripping with sorrow.

For the remainder of the journey through Squalor Keep's maintenance passages, the Summoned One was uncharacteristically silent. It was not until they reached a sliding door at the end of a long hall that he spoke again.

"Before reaching the lord's lab," the Summoned One said, "we must pass through the Cathedral of the Turtle Dragon. She is a fierce beast. I will go first."

They exited the maintenance passage into a beautifully constructed cathedral. The far wall was covered in a large, colorful mosaic depicting epic battles between brave knights and an ominous turtle dragon.

"Is that the fierce beast?" Odette asked aloud.

She pointed to the center of the room where a giant shell and skeleton of a turtle dragon lay.

"I don't think it is going to hurt anyone now," Pryvyd said.

"What happened?!" the Summoned One exclaimed, distraught. "Silvermoon was a magnificent creature when we brought her here."

"Did you forget to feed her?" Wily asked.

"She . . . she was going to have her belly filled by the burglemeisters and warriors who came to plunder the keep," the Summoned One said defensively.

"Then maybe you should have made it a little easier to get this deep." Wily added, "Who's your trapsmith?"

"Trapsmith?" The Summoned One thought about the question. "I don't think the lord had one."

"That would be your problem," Wily concluded.

The group walked past the dragon bones and through a giant door into a workshop. Wily was instantly in awe of everything inside.

It was as if someone had taken his worktable back in Carrion Tomb and expanded it into an entire room. There were thousands of hammers and wrenches lined up in neat rows, and iron, bronze, and silver gears displayed on racks for easy grabbing. There was even a quick-pump grease dispenser for speedy access.

And the tables. Oh, the tables. Each one housed a different contraption. It was easy to deduce the purpose of some of the devices, while others were so foreign in appearance that Wily would need to get his hands on them to truly understand their function.

"Lord! It is I, the Summoned One."

There was no response.

Moshul, being much taller than the rest of the group, pointed to something behind one of the tall tool shelves and signed to Odette and Pryvyd.

"Moshul thinks he knows where your lord is," Pryvyd said to the Summoned One.

Moshul led the group to a cage shaped like a dome. Wily recognized the design; it was much like the first stage of his Wake-No-More. The curved sides of the cage would spring up from the floor and snap together to capture a person should they set foot in it.

And it wasn't empty. The skeleton of a man was locked inside, his skeletal arms reaching for a set of keys just out of grasp on a nearby (but not near enough) table.

"I think that might be why your lord never came to check on you," Pryvyd said, putting a sympathetic hand on the Summoned One's shoulder. "He accidentally locked himself into his own contraption."

"Take what you want," the Summoned One said with a sigh as he dropped his head in defeat. "This has all been in vain."

"Where is the treasure?" Pryvyd asked.

"This is it," the Summoned One said. "There is no gold or diamonds here. The most valuable treasures of the Gromanov family were these inventions. They are what has the power to truly change this land."

Pryvyd looked around at the half-finished inventions with a frown. Clearly he was not pleased.

"None of this will help get us to the Salt Isles," Pryvyd said.

"This might," Odette said as she moved across the room to a glass case filled with a glowing fist-size stone inside.

"What is it?" Wily asked aloud.

"I don't know," Odette responded. "But if something glows and is stored in a glass case, it's bound to be important."

"I can't say I know what it is either." The Summoned One added, "The lord was very selective about what he told me."

Pryvyd walked over to Odette to examine the stone. Wily was about to join them when an open book caught his eye. The pages were filled with blueprints and step-by-step instructions on how to build complicated machines. He flipped the pages and recognized some of the objects within—he had built crude versions of them in his sleeping chamber at the Carrion Tomb. Yet others were objects far beyond his understanding.

The Summoned One had turned away from Odette and Pryvyd and was watching Wily examine the book.

"Take it," the snake man said. "I'm sure my lord would be happy that you were interested. It was written by his favorite author."

Wily tucked it under his arm as he headed back to the group. Odette was carefully placing the glowing stone in her wooden puzzle box.

"Shall I guide you out?" the Summoned One asked.

THE GROUP EXITED Squalor Keep and stepped through the illusionary hillside. Above, the moon was just a sliver, like the curved blade of a hobgoblet's throwing knife. The Summoned One breathed in the night air.

"Good luck on your travels to the Salt Isles," he said.

"You can come with us," Roveeka offered.

"I'm heading north where there are more of my kind," the snake man said as he slithered off. "Farewell."

After watching him depart, Odette turned to the others with the puzzle box in hand.

"The Floating City is not far from here. And if there's something to be sold, that's the place to find a buyer."

After a brief glance at her map, Odette led the way south through the maze of jagged rocks. Pryvyd and Wily walked side-by-side behind her, with Moshul and Roveeka bringing up the rear.

"I see you found yourself a souvenir," Pryvyd said with a smile. "And you wasted no time writing your name on it."

Wily looked confused. He couldn't write anything, including his own name.

"What are you talking about?" Wily asked.

"On the cover of that book you're holding," Pryvyd clarified, "it reads 'Wily Snare's Book of Inventions.'"

13

THE FLOATING CITY

As Wily walked through tufts of gravel grass, he let his finger trace the raised letters on the cover of the leather-bound book.

Why is my name on the cover of this book? Could Wily Snare be the name of the author, or perhaps the name of the dead lord of Squalor Keep? Is it just an unbelievable coincidence? Or did this book somehow belong to me?

"Are we nearly there?" Roveeka asked from Moshul's shoulders, interrupting Wily's racing thoughts. "I'm exhausted."

"You're the only one *not* walking," Pryvyd said, surprised. "How can you be tired?"

"Baby slither trolls fall asleep easier on their father's backs," Odette said.

"Are you calling me a baby?" Roveeka asked, offended.

"No," Odette replied. "You're just acting like one."

"Let me down," Roveeka said to Moshul, fuming.

The moss golem held onto her leg to stop her from climbing to the ground.

"The spot where we'll stop for the night is not far from here," Pryvyd said to calm the situation.

Wily had discovered that "not far from here" (a phrase that both Odette and Pryvyd used often) meant something different to them than it did to Wily. Back in the tomb, "not far from here" meant one chamber away or a hundred steps at the most. But everything in the Above was so huge, "not far from here" could mean a two-days' walk. Even when you saw something in the distance, it could take hours or more to reach it. Wily really wished they hadn't left the horses behind in Vale Village.

By midnight, they had arrived at the top of the grassy hill where they would make their camp. While it was not in any way hidden from prying eyes, it did have the advantage of being in a location where no one would be able to sneak up on them.

All the blankets and sleeping gear had been lost to

the torn everstuff satchel, but it didn't bother Roveeka and Pryvyd, who both fell asleep quickly in the grass. Odette had taken a seat on a rock and was fingering her puzzle box as she stared into the distance. Wily got up from the cold ground and approached her.

"Of all the things in the everstuff satchel," Wily said, "why'd you grab that box?"

"It's unbreakable," Odette said as she continued to gaze toward the dark horizon. "You can't smash it open. You have to take care to unlock its secrets. Know the right combination or be smart enough, like you, to fig-ure it out. My mother told me that there wouldn't be very many able to do that."

For a moment Wily thought he heard a crack in her voice. Then she hopped off the rock.

"You should get some sleep," Odette said. "Tomorrow will be no easier than today."

BEFORE WILY EVEN opened his eyes, he felt the ground beneath him give way. Waking with a start, he tried to scramble to safety as the hillside started collapsing in on itself. He made a flying leap to try to grab Moshul's outstretched hand, but instead found himself falling.

Frantically, Wily reached out and caught hold of

a sprig of dead roots sticking out of the mud. He was dangling, kicking away crumbling clumps of dirt as he scrambled to find purchase. Above, he could see Moshul, Pryvyd, and Odette looking down at him from the edge of the hole. They called out for him, but their voices were too distant to hear.

With no warning, the clump of roots slipped loose, tugging free from the dirt, sending Wily falling. . . .

When he hit the ground, he managed to land on his feet. He looked around and realized he was in a tunnel he knew too well.

He was back in the entrance corridor of Carrion Tomb. The circle of blue sky glimmered brightly at the end of it. Wily turned to run for it, but managed only a few steps before something grabbed his ankle. He looked down to see a muddy oglodyte's hand wrapped tightly around his foot, its nails digging into his flesh. As soon as he tried to kick himself free, another hand reached out from the ground and snagged his other foot.

Hundreds of rats poured out of holes in the tunnel walls.

"Where are you, Snare?" hissed a familiar voice.

Stalag emerged from the darkness. His sandaled feet crushing and cracking rat tails with every step.

"Stalag, please," Wily begged. "Let me go."

The cavern mage's quivering eyeballs cracked open and thousands of tiny spiders burst forth, crawling all over the cavern mage's face. Then from his cracked, bloody lips—

"I told you to call me . . . Father," Stalag whispered.

Wily snapped awake. It was still night. He felt something prickly on his neck. He looked down to see a tiny spider, just like the one from his dream, crawl down his sleeve and disappear into the grass.

THE REST OF the trip to the Floating City was downhill, which was a welcome break for everyone's legs. As the city came into view, Wily realized how it had gotten its name. It wasn't just a large town on the edge of the lake, but an enormous maze of boats and rafts tied together with buildings and roads built atop. A long, wooden bridge stretched from the shore to the arched welcome gate of the city. Hundreds of carts and carriages were collected on the lake's bank. It appeared only foot traffic was permitted in the city.

"Let's be sure to stick close together," Pryvyd said. "The patrons and residents of the Floating City are not known for their honesty."

Even before reaching the bridge, merchants approached Wily and the others trying to peddle their wares.

"I got the rings and amulets you're after," a short, hairy gwarf implored.

"Poisons here," offered a silver-winged squatling no taller than Wily's knee. "Sleeping, deadly, and worse for your not-drinking pleasure. Make your enemies wish they dined with someone else."

Wily pushed past the flightless fairy as she shook small jars of poison with her three-fingered hands, causing them to bubble and fizz.

"Elixirs for the pretty lady," a hobgoblet said to Roveeka. "A free taste for you."

"Oh thank you," Roveeka replied.

She reached out a clawed hand to grab the small golden vial, but Odette slapped her hand away.

"It's a scam," Odette admonished. "You drink a drop and you'll be transformed into a sludge lobster or something. Then they'll make us pay for the antidote to turn you back."

The hobgoblet grumbled and wandered off to find the next unsuspecting mark.

The bridge was held afloat by hundreds of large barrels just like the ones that stored the fungus beer back in Carrion Tomb. They each bobbed gently as Wily stepped from one to the next. Behind him, Moshul was so heavy that the barrels sank under the water, submerging his feet in the emerald lake water.

As they stepped onto the entrance raft of the city, Odette turned to the others.

"The first thing we need to do is find the Great Stein Tavern," she said. "There's a bounty hunter who hangs there who should be able to help."

"Find?" Wily asked. "I thought you said you'd been here hundreds of times."

"I have," Odette answered. "And I've eaten many meals in the Great Stein Tavern. But one of the interesting challenges of the Floating City is that they are constantly rearranging it. Buildings that were on one side of town could be smack dab in the middle of it the next day. It makes it difficult for visitors to get around, but also very easy to hide if you don't want to be found."

Odette approached an elf with a pushcart full of caged frakdragons, winged snails with sharp claws and sharper teeth. The elf had frizzy green hair that was singed at the ends and a pair of hooks where her hands used to be.

"We're looking for Great Stein Tavern," Odette said.

"What's it worth to you?" the hook-handed elf asked as one of her frakdragons coughed up flames.

"Ten gold pieces," Odette replied.

She dropped the coins into the elf's shirt pocket.

"Straight down Raft Alley and make a left at the axe shop."

"What if I told you it was worth twenty gold pieces to me?" Odette asked.

She dropped another ten coins in the elf's pocket.

"Then I'd give you the right directions," the dragon merchant said with a chipped-tooth smile. "Go down Raft Alley until you see the Iron Anchor and then veer to the right. Pass the row of stichems and you'll come right to it. That is assuming you make it there before high noon."

"It's a shift day?" Pryvyd asked.

"Indeed," the hook-handed elf answered. "Now, can I interest you in a frakdragon? Well trained. I lost my hand so you don't have to."

The elf gestured to a frakdragon that was chewing through the metal bars of the cage.

"Very good price," the elf offered.

Pryvyd shook his head and Odette signaled the others to follow her.

As the group made their way down Raft Alley, Wily watched the buildings move and bob with the slight changes in the wind. On the edge of every building and square of road were a series of ropes and pulleys that had to be the method for rearranging the layout of the city.

The thought that the city was constantly shifting was a thrill to Wily. His existence in the tomb had been a tedious drip of sameness. Now just like the Floating City's blocks, he knew his life could be rearranged in new and unexpected ways. Something about the possibility of it all made Wily want to hold his shoulders higher and let the moist breeze blow through his hair.

"Roveeka, look," Wily said. "Do you see all the pulleys on the sides of the rafts? They're using them to change the layout of the city!"

Roveeka gave him a weak smile. "I'm glad you find that exciting."

Despite his hobgoblet companion's lack of interest, Wily eyed the complicated engineering feat with amazement.

At the end of the Raft Alley was a large anchor that seemed big enough to hold a thousand boats in place.

"That used to be the anchor that held the center of the city in place," Odette explained. "Of course, that was when it was just a fraction of the size that it is now."

Wily noticed that the harsh tone that Odette usually took with him was noticeably absent. In fact, she had been downright pleasant since their quiet evening talk.

Wily could only wonder how large the anchor was that currently held the Floating City in place.

The group veered to the right as the hook-handed dragon merchant had instructed them to do. "Past the row of stichems . . . ," Odette muttered, repeating the elf's direction as she looked around the street. "Ah-ha," she said, her eyes settling on what must be the stichems working in their stalls. They were elves and gwarfs who seemed to specialize in sewing up cuts and bruises with thread. A tough-looking troll wasn't acting so tough as a stichem closed a nasty cut on his wrist.

"Make it stop," the troll whined as he covered his eyes with his free hand.

"There it is," Odette said as she pointed to a dining establishment. The steel sign hanging from the front had a picture of a mug shaped like a mountain.

Even before they walked in the front door, Wily was overwhelmed by the aroma of cooked fish. That explained the pack of alley cats lingering by the dining hall's windows.

The Great Stein Tavern had dozens of circular tables where patrons were rowdily eating and drinking. In the center of the tavern was a large hole in the floorboards that dropped directly into the lake itself. A trio of squatlings held fishing poles above the water, luring in fish with their fluttering iridescent wings. When one pulled in a large snapper, he threw it on a plate and showed it to a female customer sitting at a nearby table.

"You want it grilled and deboned or roasted with the skin?" the squatling asked with a flick of her forked tongue.

"I want it now," the female customer said, grabbing it from the plate and biting off the head.

"Over by the fireplace." Pryvyd pointed to a booth where a young man in an olive robe sat talking with a scraggly gwarf who, judging by the sutures all over his face and hands, had just paid a lot of coin to a stichem.

Odette wound her way through the tightly packed tables. Moshul knocked the backs of chairs as he moved, causing a few patrons to spill their drinks. Fortunately, no one seemed keen on messing with a moss golem.

As they got closer, the olive-robed man in the booth looked up at his soon-to-be visitors. Smile creases quickly formed in the golden skin that surrounded his beady gray eyes.

"Odette," the olive-robed man said as he scraped his dirty fingernails through his orange beard, "what dungeon have you just come stumbling out from?"

"It's nice to see you, too, Needlepocket," she said. She sounded as if she knew him well, but they weren't necessarily friends.

"What are you trying to sell off today?"

Odette stared silently at the scraggly gwarf. She wasn't going to talk with him present.

"Get out of here, Scallygump." The sunbaked bounty hunter gave the gwarf a tough push, sending him tumbling out of the booth. With a *humpf*, the gwarf grumbled away, looking rather perturbed.

Odette peered around to see who was watching them. She slid into the booth next to Needlepocket. Pryvyd and Moshul formed a wall around the table to block the view from nearby diners.

Odette reached into her pocket and pulled out the puzzle box. With a few quick motions, she opened it to reveal the glowing stone from Squalor Keep. Wily noticed the lantern near the table begin to flicker.

"Do you know who would be willing to pay for this?" Odette asked.

Needlepocket's eyes widened in amazement. He quickly shut the lid of the box, keeping his hand over it protectively.

"Where did you get this?" he asked urgently.

"We pulled it from Squalor Keep."

"Impossible," the bounty hunter insisted. "How'd you get past the first trap? I know a lot of people who lost their friends trying to pillage that one."

"We had an expert with us," Pryvyd said, looking over to Wily.

"Never mind how we got it," Odette interrupted. "How much do you think this is worth, and who would be willing to pay for it?"

"Few have the gold to afford this," Needlepocket said. "It's worth more than a donkey cart of diamonds."

The olive-robed bounty hunter peered over his shoulder and eyed the room, making sure that no one was eavesdropping on their conversation. Only after he was certain did he speak again.

"This is a Sun Stone," Needlepocket said in a hushed tone. "Few even know of their existence. They are what power the great machines of the land. There is one at the heart of the Infernal Fortress and one inside the great prisonaut. The King himself has been looking for a third."

"We're not selling it to the Infernal King," Pryvyd said curtly.

"He wouldn't want to pay for it," Needlepocket corrected. "He'd just rip it out of your hands."

Suddenly, the lantern near the table stopped flickering. A small winged creature emerged from the flames and shot toward the exit. It was the same creature that the Scarf had pulled from the gearfolk back in Vale Village.

"A rust fairy!" Pryvyd said with alarm.

Righteous tried to pluck it out of the air, but the creature was too quick. It escaped through an open window, its wings flapping so quickly they blurred.

"And you think I'm out of shape," Pryvyd muttered to Righteous as he flew back.

Righteous flashed Pryvyd a disparaging pinky.

"Damn rust fairies are all over the city," Needlepocket said. "They're everywhere, spying for the Infernal King. Nowhere's safe from their tiny eyes. Once it tells the gearfolk that you have a Sun Stone, they will be here within minutes. As long as you have this in your possession, you'll be the most wanted people in all of Panthasos."

Needlepocket was talking so quickly and quietly that Wily could barely keep up with the conversation, especially with his heart now pounding loudly.

"Who will pay for this?" Odette said urgently.

"I'd have to ask around," Needlepocket replied. "For how much would you be willing to part with it?"

"Safe passage to the Salt Isles," Pryvyd said.

"There's a merchant by the name of Thrush

Flannigan who lives in Ratgull Harbor. He'd be willing to make that trade."

The loud clang of rattling metal could be heard outside.

"The gearfolk are already here," Needlepocket said. "You need to leave now."

Wily spun to face the door, but he didn't see any of the mechanical men standing there. At least not yet.

"Is there a back door?" Pryvyd asked.

"Only one door," Needlepocket replied. "But there is another way out. I hope you can all swim."

The robed bounty hunter got up from his table and ran for the fishing pool in the center of the restaurant.

"Deep breath!" he shouted to the others behind him as he dove into the pool.

Wily was suddenly very glad he had spent all those hours at the bottom of the underground lake, scraping algae off the sunken rocks.

Pryvyd and Roveeka jumped in next, followed by Moshul, who made such a large splash that it soaked everyone in the tavern. Wily stepped to the edge of the tavern floor just as one of the wheeled gearfolk bashed open the door.

Wily took a deep breath and jumped into the lake.

14

CRACKED MOON

The water sent a chilling blast of energy through Wily's chest. With eyes open, he could see the others in front of him swimming through the dark green waters. Shafts of light shined through between the gaps in the interconnected boats.

Wily paddled as fast as he could, his lungs tightening from lack of air. Ahead, he saw the others rising to the surface where there was a small square opening. It was so tight a squeeze that Moshul was barely able to make it through.

A hand reached down into the water, waiting to pull Wily out.

He was tugged to the surface by Needlepocket. Wily

gulped air greedily and, after wiping the lake water from his eyes, looked around. He was in a laundry room where a group of gwarven explorers were scrubbing their dirty pantaloons.

But Wily was most surprised to see Needlepocket still holding firmly to his arm. The bounty hunter was staring at the exposed burn mark visible beneath the wet sleeve bunched up around Wily's elbow. He looked at it closely as if it were the most shocking thing in the world.

"How did you get this mark?" Needlepocket asked urgently as Odette pulled herself out of the water behind him.

"I don't know," Wily said. "I've had it since as long as I can remember. The mage of the tomb told me the sun burned my skin. But I know that's a lie."

"Fourteen years ago," Needlepocket said, "a shrouded woman came to me with a mission: to find a missing toddler. A toddler who had a distinctive burn on his arm in the shape of a cracked moon. Just like this one."

Needlepocket reached into his shirt and removed a sealed tube and popped the cap. He pulled out a dry piece of paper and unfurled it. Wily looked down to see a picture of his scar drawn there.

"My parents?" Wily said, choking up.

The bounty hunter nodded.

"Your mother. She told me to hang a lantern in the famed Crawlin' Tree of the Twighast Forest when I found her son and wait there for her to arrive."

Wily could barely breathe. He was drowning in the beating of his own heart. Roveeka trudged over to his side and gave him a joyous hug.

"This is amazing!" she exclaimed.

Moshul signed to Pryvyd, but the knight was too busy staring at Wily to answer the golem.

"Am I the only one who remembers where we are right now?" Odette called from the door to the laundry room. "It won't take the gearfolk long to figure out where we went. We need to get back to the main bridge before they close it off."

"I'll get you out of the city," Needlepocket said.

"You'll come with us?" Odette said, surprised.

"If I get this boy to the Crawlin' Tree," the bounty hunter said, "I'll be able to buy myself a castle. She was offering a hefty reward."

"We're not going to the Crawlin' Tree," Odette said.

"Let's discuss this later," Pryvyd added urgently.

The group, led by Needlepocket, exited the laundry building and found themselves in a grimy promenade constructed of waterlogged rafts.

"This way," Needlepocket said, leading them in the opposite direction of the shore.

Moshul began signing frantically and pointing the other way.

"But the bridge is in the other direction!" Pryvyd said, seeming to second what Moshul was saying.

"Which is why they'd expect us to head that way," Needlepocket said.

There was no time for debate. The group followed the bounty hunter. Wily lagged behind the rest of the group, even Roveeka.

"Come on, brother," Roveeka called back to him.

His feet may not have been moving quickly, but Wily's mind was racing. *My mother was looking for me?* Every other step he glanced down at the burn mark on his arm. *Is she still looking for me?* He could only half pay attention to every sharp turn they took from boat to boat. *Could I actually find her?*

As they passed a row of fish stalls, Wily could hear a distant bell ringing.

"Noon already?" Pryvyd said, panting.

"This is going to get more difficult," Odette stated.

It took only a moment for Wily to realize why. The entire city started to shift. The streets and buildings began to interlock and slide like pieces of a block puzzle.

The ropes and pulleys on the side of every raft came to life, squeaking and turning.

The road they were running down suddenly had a cheese shop in the middle of it, and the street they were planning to continue down was drifting away.

"We need to wait for the shift to stop," Pryvyd said. "Otherwise we will only be getting ourselves further lost."

"Found them!"

The high-pitched scream came from behind. Wily looked over his shoulder to see a gearfolk scout rolling toward them with a long hook stick.

"Hand over the Sun Stone," the gearfolk scout called out to the group, "and I will tell the Infernal King that you cooperated."

"I'll handle this," Needlepocket said.

The bounty hunter grabbed a wooden billy club from his robe and charged the gearfolk.

"I need reinforcements!" the gearfolk scout screamed as Needlepocket sped toward him.

The gearfolk was about to scream again when his head was knocked off by a trident. Needlepocket stopped in his tracks, surprised.

Wily was shocked, too. It hadn't been any of his companions who had thrown the weapon.

"That wassssh a per-ef-ect hit!" Agorop called out to his sister.

From around the corner, six oglodytes, including Agorop and Sceely, emerged with tridents and blades in hand.

Needlepocket turned to face the oglodytes.

"I don't know who you think you are," he said, "but this bounty is mine."

A bolt of crackling black energy flew through the air and struck Needlepocket in the chest. Roveeka and Pryvyd gasped as he was sent flying off the road and into the water.

Wily knew who had to be steps behind the oglodytes.

"Give me back the boy!" Stalag said from beneath the dark cloak that was covering his head and body. "I promise I won't hurt you in return."

"You said we could get all killy and the like!" Sceely whined.

"I said *I* wouldn't hurt them," Stalag said with wicked satisfaction. "Never mentioned what you'd be doing."

"You can't control me anymore," Wily shouted to Stalag.

"Don't talk to your father that way," the cavern mage hissed.

"I'm not your son," Wily said. "You kidnapped me."

"The Above has made you arrogant and disrespectful. Bite your tongue."

The oglodytes were slowly but purposefully moving toward them with weapons tightly gripped in their webbed hands. Moshul, Pryvyd, and Righteous prepared for battle. Roveeka pulled out her knives. Odette tightened her fists.

"Who's been hindgeezered now?" Sceely said. (This was yet another oglodyte word for ambushing, specifically meaning "to back into a corner and poke with sharp sticks.")

Wily looked over his shoulder. The cheese shop that had formed the dead end was moving. In a moment, he and his companions would have a path to escape.

"There's nowhere you can go that I won't find you," Stalag said.

Behind Wily, the dead end had cleared. There was now a clear path to . . . a junk barge.

The oglodytes snickered to themselves as Wily and his friends backed their way onto yet another trap.

"We'll never be able to outswim the oglodytes," Roveeka stammered, looking into the lake. "They're faster than fish."

Wily wasn't looking in the water. He was scanning the junk barge, eyeing the pieces of metal and wood littered across it. Swords, gears, a ship's wheel, a broken mop—

"Can you hold them off for two minutes . . . maybe three?" Wily asked.

"We'll fight them off as long as we can," Pryvyd said.

"So you can tinker?" Odette asked as she stretched her muscles, preparing for the onslaught of oglodytes.

Wily reached down into a pile of scrap metal and began pulling out old swords, searching for six that were roughly the same size.

A pair of oglodyte tridents flew toward Pryvyd, but Righteous knocked them out of the air before they could even nick the knight's armor.

"I had that covered," Pryvyd shouted to Righteous.

The floating arm ignored his former body.

"Don't hurt Wily," Stalag commanded. "I need him unharmed."

Satisfied with a half-dozen rusty broadswords he had found in a barrel, Wily turned his attention to an old ship's steering wheel that he discovered tossed in the corner of the barge. He pulled his trusty hammer and screwdriver from his trapsmith belt and set to work attaching the blades onto the outside of the wheel.

"Back in the tomb," Wily explained aloud, "I tried building an underwater chop-o-lot."

Stalag arched his hands, sending two arrows of crackling black energy at Pryvyd. The bolts hit the knight in the chest, causing him to drop his spiked shield. Stalag was about to fire two more arrows of energy when Needlepocket emerged from the water behind him and tackled the cavern mage.

"I said, that's my bounty!" Needlepocket growled.

A pair of oglodytes grabbed the bounty hunter by the shoulders and pulled him off Stalag.

"Chop-o-lot?" Odette asked, not having the faintest idea what Wily was doing.

"It's a spinning blade trap that never worked the way I had hoped it would."

An oglodyte came charging for the junk barge. With a powerful roundhouse kick, Odette smacked the oglodyte in the face.

"And you're going to try to get it right now?" Odette said, clearly thinking this was a very bad idea.

"No," Wily stated. "I'm going to try to get it wrong again."

Odette stole a glance at the steering wheel, which now had three broadswords sticking out from it like flower petals.

"Maybe the sun is finally melting your brain."

Sceely, seizing the opportunity, came running toward

Pryvyd with her trident. But just before she could strike him, Mum flew through the air and knocked her in the head. Roveeka had saved Pryvyd just in time.

"Good throw," Pryvyd complimented Roveeka.

"It was all Mum!" Roveeka said modestly as she ran to retrieve her precious dagger.

Wily attached the last three blades to the wheel, completing the metallic flower. Then he grabbed a fistful of gears and the broken mop.

"A little longer," Wily called to the others.

Two of the oglodytes charged Moshul. The moss golem knocked one of them into the water and another through the window of an inn.

Stalag began mumbling to himself. Wily knew the mage was casting a spell. At once, Agorop began to grow in size until he was taller than Moshul.

"I'm mush bigger then every-a-body!" Agorop shouted through his now dragon-size rows of razor-sharp teeth.

Agorop threw a punch at Moshul, knocking the moss golem in the jaw and sending him tumbling back. Moshul nearly stepped on Roveeka.

"Might not be able to hold them back as long as we expected," Pryvyd said.

Wily interlocked a chain of gears, connecting the wheel to the broken mop handle. He gave the handle a spin—it served to crank the wheel around. He was nearly done. He just needed to mount it onto the back of the barge.

Righteous rocketed through the air with his sword clutched in his bronze gauntlet. But Stalag was prepared. He unleashed a tornado of wind that sent the arm spinning like a salamander drowning in a whirlpool.

"There," Wily said, having finished his flower of swords. "Now I just attach it to this crank. . . ."

"I think your old friends are too smart to walk into that," Odette said as she chopped an oglodyte with the back of her hand.

But Wily placed the circle of blades into the water and bolted the base of the steering wheel to the side of the junk barge.

"Everyone on the barge!" Wily yelled. "Moshul, I need you to turn this crank as fast as you can."

Odette bounded onto the boat. "What's that going to do?" she worried aloud.

Moshul moved to the back of the barge and grabbed the mop handle of Wily's makeshift invention. And he turned it with all his might.

The entire barge lurched forward. Pryvyd had to leap to the junk barge as it started to move away. Righteous, who was still battling back the oglodytes as they tried to board the boat, flew onto the barge as well.

Pryvyd looked at the invention Wily had built with amazement.

"A self-propelled boat!" Pryvyd said in awe. "It's like magic."

The barge moved faster and faster as Moshul cranked harder. Wily stuck a long stick into the water at the back of the boat.

"Pryvyd, hold on to this and use it as a rudder," Wily said.

Pryvyd snatched it in his left hand and steered the fast-moving junk barge away from the floating city.

From the alley raft, Wily could hear Stalag shouting to his minions.

"Follow them!"

Three of the oglodytes, including the enlarged one, jumped into the lake and tried to catch up. But with Moshul cranking so speedily it was impossible for them to keep pace.

The junk barge sped across the lake as Wily watched Stalag shrink into the distance.

"I guess you can build more than traps," Pryvyd said, impressed.

But despite nearly being killed by the gearfolk and captured by Stalag, Wily still had only one thing on his mind: the mystery of his past. How did the scar on his arm, the woman who had been searching for him, and the book of inventions all fit together?

15

THE PUZZLE BOX

The junk barge cracked and snapped the dense thorn reeds standing guard along the far side of the lake. As they neared the muddy shore, Moshul stopped cranking the chop-o-lot and let the barge slowly pull to a stop in the swampy mire.

With a short running start, Odette handspringed off the front of the barge. She landed solidly on the dry earth without getting her shoes dirty.

"Show off," Roveeka said as she slid out of the barge and into the thick, wet mud.

By the time Wily had trudged his way to shore, Odette was already tracing her finger along one of the maps from her scroll tube.

"If we can purchase horses in the next town," Odette said to Pryvyd, "it should take us only three or four days at the most to reach Ratgull Harbor."

"But first we're going to the Crawlin' Tree," Wily interjected.

Odette nearly laughed at the suggestion.

"No," she said. "That's not part of the plan."

"Well, I say it is."

"I get it," Pryvyd said kindly. "The woman who was looking for you could have been your mother. But that was more than a decade ago. You can't expect her to still be checking that tree."

"I have to know for sure," Wily said insistently.

Odette was bristling at the suggestion.

"Then go," she said plainly. "You did your part. You got us through Squalor Keep. Although I'm guessing that once you get yourself stuck in the Infernal King's prisonaut, you'll wish you'd gone with us."

Odette turned away coldly. Wily's heart sank at her callous response.

"I can't make it there alone," Wily said, hoping it would change her mind.

"I'm sure your hobgoblet half sis will stick by your side," Odette replied without facing him.

"Of course I will," Roveeka said, holding her humped

shoulders high. Wily felt a rush of affection for her—he knew he could always count on Roveeka's support. Then, turning to Wily, she whispered, "I think I could convince Moshul to come with us. And I certainly won't miss the elf."

"I do need your help," Wily said in an impassioned plea to Odette, Moshul, and Pryvyd. "It's too dangerous out here for just the two of us. You know the roads and the shortcuts and the threats that I'll never recognize until it is too late."

The truth was that, in addition to appreciating their talents, he had begun to care for them. He didn't want to lose these new friends he had only just made.

Pryvyd looked over sympathetically to Odette, who remained stone-faced as Wily continued.

"I promise that if we get to the tree and we don't find the woman Needlepocket told us about, I will come with you and help you raid every dungeon until the end of time. I'm begging you."

Odette stood there with a thoughtful look on her face. Then she spoke.

"Nope," Odette said. "Not going to happen. We're going to Ratgull Harbor. No more discussion."

"I was afraid you might say that," Wily responded with a sigh of disappointment.

"You're going to be thanking me once we are halfway across the ocean, relaxing on the back of a sailing ship."

"And how do you plan on paying for the trip?" Wily asked simply.

Odette didn't like Wily's blank stare.

"What did you do with the Sun Stone?" she said as she began to fumble through her side pouch.

She pulled the puzzle box out, and in a panic, gave it a shake. Inside, she heard the rattle of the Sun Stone rolling against the sides of the hidden inner compartment.

"The stone is still in there," Odette said confidently. Then she began to doubt her own statement. "Or something's in there."

"The stone is still inside," Wily said. "But you're not going to be able to get it out."

Odette quickly slid her hands along the outside of the box, trying to unlock it. But there was something different. The pieces were not moving the way they usually did. Wily could see her anger rising.

"I changed the combination while we were crossing the lake," Wily said. "I slipped the box out of your pouch while you weren't paying attention."

"Open it now," Odette demanded, shoving the box in Wily's face.

"Not until we get to the Crawlin' Tree."

Odette handed the box to Moshul.

"Moshul will smash it open," she said as if she had solved the problem.

"Remember what you told me," Wily stated. "The box is unbreakable. That Sun Stone is in there until I let it out."

Odette pulled it back from Moshul.

"I lied," Odette said. "An enchanted gwarven hammer could bust it open."

"And most likely shatter the Sun Stone inside," Roveeka countered. "Trust me. I know rocks."

Pryvyd actually seemed amused.

"Looks like you finally met someone as tricky as you," Pryvyd said to Odette. "Not so much fun being fooled, is it?"

Odette was fuming. This was not an elf who enjoyed having her hand forced.

"You betrayed me," Odette said, giving Wily a deadly stare.

"I just wanted you to come with me!" Wily snapped back.

"The Crawlin' Tree is in the haunted Twighast Forest," Odette said through clenched teeth. "It's a day's journey in the other direction. All the while, Stalag will still be searching for you."

"I'm not changing my mind," Wily said, determined.

"You need to know when you've been beat," Pryvyd said to Odette.

"And Wily and I beat you," Roveeka said, clearly enjoying the moment.

Odette shoved the box back into Wily's hands and started walking in the opposite direction of Ratgull Harbor.

"Those stupid acorns could have told us to find any trapsmith," Odette mumbled to herself. "Why'd they have to pick him?"

"She holds a grudge," Pryvyd said to Wily and Roveeka before following after Odette. "Be prepared for that."

EVERY OTHER STEP it seemed as if Wily was swatting a biting insect from his neck, ankle, or ears. They had been following the edge of the lake for hours and the ground had been getting softer and wetter with every mile traveled. Even worse, a swarm of mosquitoes, flies, and weltwings was following Moshul as if he were some newly discovered parcel of swamp they needed to take residence in.

"Moshul," Odette said, waving him away, "keep your distance."

The moss golem shot her a bunch of angry hand gestures.

"They may not be biting you," Odette responded. "But they're eating me alive."

"They don't seem to be bothering me," Roveeka interjected from Moshul's shoulders.

"That's because hobgoblet skin is too thick for them to get their stingers into," Odette replied.

"It's good to be me," Roveeka said.

Odette shot a quick glance at Wily. Not a friendly one.

"Moshul," Odette added, "maybe you can go and walk next to Wily. Let them eat him instead."

As the sun started to dip behind the mountains, Pryvyd told everyone they should begin searching for a safe place to camp for the night.

"What's wrong with right here?" Roveeka said, looking around at the small patch of dry land they were now standing on.

"This is crab-dragon country," Pryvyd said. "They skitter out from their mud holes at night and look for food. It's best that we keep moving until we find someplace protected."

"Like that hill up ahead," Odette said, shifting direction slightly to head for a large uneven mound of earth in the distance.

As they got closer, Wily could see that what they were heading for was not made of earth or stone. It was a giant steel building sunk into the muck.

"It's a fallen prisonaut," Pryvyd said.

Seeing one up close left Wily's jaw hanging open in awe. The walls were a hundred feet high with sharpened spikes and twisted razor wire that would keep even the most skilled climber from making it over the top. One of the giant wheels that it had once rolled upon barely stuck out of the mire. The guard towers had long since been abandoned, and only thin strings of green-and-yellow cloth dangled from them, limply swaying in the barely-there breeze.

The prisonaut's metal gate had either rotted off its hinges or had been torn from them, as it now lay like a welcome mat before the open archway.

"Stay behind me," Pryvyd said as he drew his weapon from his sheath. "Who knows what could have taken up residence inside."

Stepping through the entranceway, Wily was shocked by what he saw. He had expected rows and rows of cages where the prisoners would be housed, each with a lock dangling from the door. Instead, it resembled a town square, complete with a fountain and steel statue of the armored Infernal King atop a snagglecart.

As they moved farther inside, Wily was able to see into the small cottages surrounding the square. One cottage looked like it was a sleeping establishment with rows of beds. The next cottage had tables and chairs inside like a restaurant. Farther along, the cottages held books, musical instruments, and even toys.

"I thought this was a moving prison," Wily said. "Where are all the cages?"

"The Infernal King doesn't think of the prisonauts as prisons at all," Pryvyd said. "He calls them his mobile villages. He thinks these are gifts to the people of Panthasos.

"This was not constructed to punish," Pryvyd continued. "It was built to control. The Infernal King hates the chaos of the world outside. The unpredictability of it all. He likes everything in its place. Machines are consistent. They do the same thing every time they are turned on. But people are not so reliable. Every day a person wakes up, they can either do the same thing they did the day before or they can decide to do something completely different.

"These moving cities were built to take those choices

away. A prison doesn't need cages to make you feel trapped. If you take away a person's choices, they could be in the most beautiful place in the world and still be caged."

Wily thought about the invaders he had captured in Carrion Tomb. At the time, he'd thought he was giving them a more productive life, but, in fact, he realized now that he was stealing something much more valuable from them: their freedom.

He had never realized just how special it was until now. He had spent his entire life being told what to do by somebody else. His decision to head for the Crawlin' Tree felt like he had finally fit a key into a lock that he had never been able to open before. He knew he might not find what he was looking for, but at least he had made this choice on his own.

Suddenly, Righteous took off across the square. It struck the outside wall of one of the restaurants, pinning a jacket and the man inside it to the wood paneling.

"Please don't hurt me," the stranger said as he tried to pull the jacket from his body, his terrified eyes darting to the disembodied arm pinning him. "I swear allegiance to the Infernal King."

At his words, the entire group's stance shifted. Pryvyd's hand tightened on his spiked shield and Odette bent her knees as if she were preparing to spring into a flip. Even Moshul's jeweled eyes narrowed.

"Is that so?" Odette asked. "We have no love for the king."

The stranger let out a long sigh of relief.

"Thank the great lair beasts for that," the mud-caked stranger said. "I hate the Infernal King, too."

"And we're supposed to believe you?" Pryvyd asked.

"No," the stranger said. "I wouldn't trust me either."

Righteous tightened his grip on the man.

"The name's Pilfish," the man said. "And this is my home. At least it has been for the last five years."

"Doesn't seem like the best spot to live," Roveeka said.

"I'm having a bit of trouble with the law of the land," Pilfish said. "The king thinks I've been stealing gold and weapons from his storehouses."

Pryvyd's grip on his sword relaxed.

"Why would he think that?" Wily asked.

"Because I have been," Pilfish said with a twisted smile. "But just enough to survive. He took everything that belonged to me and my family. Doesn't seem fair that I can't borrow a bit back from him."

Pilfish offered forth a clay jug to Pryvyd. Righteous pushed him forcefully back to the wall.

"I found some pickled leeches in the dining hall. I'd be willing to share."

"No thanks," Pryvyd said. "We just want to sleep here for the night."

Pilfish seemed to be taking extra interest in Pryvyd, staring at him long and hard.

"Do I know you?" Pilfish asked. "Did you live in here back when it was on wheels?"

"Can't say that I did," Pryvyd replied.

"The arm, of course," Pilfish said, as if suddenly solving a riddle asked by a floating skull. "You're the knight that fought the Infernal King in a one-on-one duel. You're Pryvyd Rucka."

Wily looked at Pryvyd with amazement, but Pryvyd didn't seem eager to talk about old times.

"I was there," Pilfish continued. "Not close up. But I saw it all happen. You pulled your sword on him. Had him cornered against the wall of the Infernal Fortress. He begged for mercy and you gave it to him. You told him you would let him live if he relinquished the throne. Then that spinning blade popped out of his armor and chopped your arm clean off."

Odette seemed just as amazed as Wily. It was clear she had never heard this story either. Righteous released his grip on Pilfish and hovered back to Pryvyd's side.

"If that hadn't happened—" Pilfish said.

"But it did," Pryvyd interjected.

"There would be no Infernal King."

Wily, Roveeka, Moshul, and Odette all looked to Pryvyd for his response. Righteous especially seemed to hang on his next words.

"I'm a different man now. I'm no longer shackled by a pledge to protect the land."

Wily watched Righteous slump. It put the sword it was holding back into Pryvyd's sheath and floated away.

"Give me a break," Pryvyd called out to Righteous. "You knew what I had become a long time ago. Don't pretend you didn't. I'm a thief, not a hero."

Righteous continued to drift to the far side of the prisonaut.

"If you don't like me, go find yourself a different body to hang around," Pryvyd shouted to his arm. Then he turned to the group. "What?"

Pryvyd walked off, leaving the others behind.

At Odette's request, Pilfish showed Wily, Roveeka, and her to the sleeping building. Many of the beds were still made with sheets and covers. Only a thin layer of dust rested atop them.

Wily sat down on the edge of a bed and felt the soft

springs curve under him. Wily had slept on only one bed his entire life and it felt nothing like this.

Roveeka took the bed next to his and flopped back onto it.

"It feels like I'm lying on top of a tray of jellied worm guts."

Wily lay down as well, putting his cheek on the soft dusty pillow.

"That's one way to think of it, I suppose."

"Wily, thanks for taking me," Roveeka said after a moment. "I like it here. And I know you could have just left me behind in Carrion Tomb."

"I should be thanking you," Wily said. "Without you, I'm not sure I would have had the courage to go on. So much of what I thought I knew has been wrong. It's all so hard to believe. You know what I mean?"

Roveeka did not reply.

"Roveeka?"

Still nothing. Wily sat up to see that Roveeka had already fallen asleep. He couldn't help but smile to himself as he lay back down. There was something very comforting about seeing Roveeka snoring beside him, no matter how loud her snores might be. It was as if everything was right in the world. And even though he knew she wasn't really his sister, he would always think of her as if she were.

As Wily closed his eyes, he thought about the same thing he wondered so many nights back in his sleeping chamber in Carrion Tomb. *If I could see my parents just one more time, what would I ask them? What would I tell them?*

And now he wondered if tomorrow he might actually find out the answers.

16

CRAWLIN' TREE

Wily squeezed his eyes tighter, holding onto the sweet early morning dream a little bit longer. He stared at the warm glowing face of a woman. Despite the fact that he couldn't quite make out her features, Wily was sure that she was his mother. Today, if everything went as planned, he would see her for real, not basked in the glossy haze of imagination.

When Wily finally opened his eyes, he found Roveeka already out of bed. He exited the sleeping building and scanned the fallen prisonaut for the others. The only person he caught sight of was Odette, who was standing high above the ground in the guard tower.

She was looking out into the distance.

"How did you get up there?" Wily shouted to her.

Odette turned to see him.

"There's a staircase through that black doorway," Odette pointed. "Just keep climbing until you get to the top."

From the high tower of the prisonaut, Wily could get a true appreciation for just how far they had walked the day before and how far their journey had already taken them. Beyond the swamp to the north, he could make out the edge of the lake and farther still the mountain range that was home to Squalor Keep. In the other direction was a long stretch of swamp that ended in a sea of leafless trees.

"That's the Twighast," Odette said. "It was once the forest of the Roamabout, a group of beast quellers that trained animals and creatures of all sizes. But that was before the Infernal King set fire to it. Now it's said that only the ghosts of those animals still reside in the Twighast. Even the trees themselves are scared to live there. The Crawlin' Tree was once the Standin' Tree. Tall and proud. It stretched its green arms into the sky, a home for the magical birds in the land. But after the fire, fear weighed it down. Legend has it that every night the Crawlin' Tree pulls its roots up from the ground and drags itself a little farther across the earth, desperately fleeing the terror of the dark spirits."

Wily, who was used to the spooky and unsettling, didn't like this story one bit. Then something occurred to him.

"You're trying to scare me," Wily said. "Get me to turn back."

Odette met his eyes for the first time since they had fought. "I sure am," she said.

"Now tell me the truth," Wily demanded. "What's the real story of the Twighast?"

"I didn't say I was lying."

A shiver shot down Wily's spine.

"It's still not too late to head for Ratgull Harbor," Odette said.

Then she turned back for the stairs, leaving Wily by himself, staring off in the direction of the haunted forest.

"When you're ready," Odette said, "we'll be waiting for you by the gate of the prisonaut."

AFTER SAYING FAREWELL to Pilfish, their trek took them to the cracked ground of the Twighast. The foul and putrid stink of the swamp was replaced by a different smell, one of burned hair and charred coal. The air hung heavy here, like it was trapped in a dungeon cave.

Even the breeze didn't dare move through this thicket of skeletal trees and tangled roots.

Pryvyd cautiously led the way while Righteous (who still seemed quite mad at him) took the rear. Roveeka clutched Mum and Pops in her hands, which she did whenever she was nervous. Even the insects that normally crawled all over Moshul's moving garden had retreated into their underground homes inside the moss golem.

"How do we find the Crawlin' Tree?" Roveeka asked.

"I think we just keep moving in the direction of the deadly chill and we should find it," Odette said, attempting to spook Roveeka and the others.

Wily wasn't going to fall for her game, despite the fact that she played it extremely well.

Moshul began signing to Wily. The moss golem made the gestures slow and simple. And to Wily's surprise, he was able to decipher the message.

Don't let her bother you.

Wily remembered the sign he had seen Odette use countless times. He moved his fingers from his chin down and outward to say thank you.

Moshul's jeweled eyes twinkled back as if he appreciated the effort.

Pryvyd pulled his spiked shield from his back and

raised it before him, cracking dead branches off the trees to clear a path for the group.

Wily eyed the trees for a single leaf or bug. Even the death crypts would have moths or spiders hidden among the bones, but just as the legend had said, Wily could not see even the tiniest source of life.

Then, in the distance, Wily could hear a RUMBLE. It was not a sound he had ever heard before.

"It sounds like a storm is rolling in," Odette said, then clarified for Wily, "Rain and thunder and lightning."

"I know what a storm is," Wily snapped back, despite the fact that he really didn't.

The rumbling was growing louder and steadier as if it were approaching quickly.

"I don't think that's a storm," Pryvyd said as the earth and trees started to rattle.

Through the thicket of charred branches, Wily could see the gray fog start to glow a pale ethereal green.

"Ghosts," Wily said under his breath as the now green fog grew more vivid.

Out of the mist, a stampede of spectral elk burst forth, beating their hooves against the ground. Their twisted antlers and hooves glowed a pale green like a bat's eye while their chests were a deep emerald like the moss on Moshul's knuckles.

Their bodies were moving through the trunks of the trees as if the thick wood was no more resistant than air. Yet somehow the elk antlers would shake the tree branches and their hooves would reverberate against the hard earth.

"They're coming right for us!" Wily shouted.

Odette leaped straight up and grabbed an overhead branch. She spun around it once before flipping to an even higher limb.

"Get up here," she called down to the rest of the group.

Wily looked around, but before he could decide where to move next, the ghostly herd of dead beasts was upon him.

The first elk struck him in the chest headfirst with its antlers. It felt like he was being stabbed with a spear. The pain shot through him—as did the elk itself. Wily was reeling in agony when the second elk struck him, knocking him to the hard ground. The next elk trampled him, its glowing hooves stomping down on his fingers and back. They were crushing his lungs, leaving him gasping for breath. Yet when Wily looked down at his body, he realized the elks had left no wounds.

As the rest of the herd trampled over him, he tried to spot his companions, but the elks' pale glowing forms clouded his vision.

"Rovee—" He couldn't even call out his sister's name. An elk stepped on his throat, muting his cry.

The pain grew as the next dozen galloped over him. Wily could only remain limp, struggling for air. He couldn't handle this much longer.

And then the elk were gone. After a moment, Wily sat up.

Roveeka and Pryvyd had been floored by the phantom herd as well. Moshul walked over to help Pryvyd to his feet. Wily and Roveeka rose shakily.

"The Twighast elk once roamed these woods in life," Pryvyd said, clutching an invisible wound on his torso. "They were the steeds and companions to the Roamabout. They tried to protect the trees from the Infernal King's fire flingers, but all of them perished in the flames. Now, even in death, they still try to protect the forest."

Odette dropped from the tree, both feet landing firmly on the ground.

"I told you to get up into the trees," Odette said with a smirk.

"If you want me to stay on your side," Pryvyd groaned, "you better watch what you say."

COMING TO A stop, Wily stared at a broken tree with a ring of bones at its base. The sight was enough to make his heart sink. They had already passed this tree not once, but twice. They were lost and going in circles.

"Does this look familiar?" Wily asked Odette.

"Trees surrounded by bones are pretty common in the Twighast," Pryvyd reassured Wily.

"But how many have a spring I left behind?" Wily asked as he bent down.

He picked up a shiny curl of metal and showed it to the others.

"Far fewer, I'm guessing," Pryvyd said.

"Don't look at me," Odette, who had been leading the group, said. "I want to get to the tree as fast as we can. The sooner we get there, the sooner we can change course for Ratgull Harbor."

"Which way were you planning on leading us from here?" Roveeka asked.

Odette pointed along a path that appeared to be covered with black snow.

"Then let's head in the opposite direction," Roveeka insisted. "You seem to be wrong about a lot of things."

Odette fumed. Wily realized that this could get ugly. But before Odette could speak, Pryvyd interjected.

"Let's give it try," the knight said. "Once you're lost, you can't get any more lost."

The group headed in the direction that Roveeka had pointed. There was very little different to see, just more dead trees and ash-covered ground. The one positive about the new direction was that it looked less familiar to Wily.

They passed through what appeared to be a dry streambed, long streaks in the earth that twisted off into the distance, rising and falling with the curves in the earth.

"At least we haven't passed this stream before," Wily said, "or what's left of a stream."

Wily suddenly felt a huge hand grab him on the shoulder. Moshul spun him around and started moving his mossy hands up and down.

"Moshul is trying to tell us something," Wily called out.

Pryvyd quickly began translating.

"He says to look how the path of the stream traveled," Pryvyd said. "Up and down over the hills."

"So?" Odette said. "Why is that important?"

Wily put the pieces together.

"Because water only travels downhill," Wily thought aloud, "never up. This isn't a dried stream."

"It's the trail of the Crawlin' Tree!" Odette said with a burst of excitement.

The elf looked down at the track marks in the ground.

"It was heading that way," she said before taking off.

Wily raced behind her, but only for a couple strides. He was moving so quickly that he found himself ahead of the elf, taking the lead.

Wily had never run so fast in all his days and nights. He was so close to the answers he had waited his whole life to discover. It was just like the moment before opening a treasure chest hidden in the deepest dungeon. Anything could be inside. Gold, jewels, or something magical. The others struggled to keep pace behind him.

As he came over the third hill, he got his first glimpse of the Crawlin' Tree. It wasn't hard to see how the tree had gotten its name. The trunk was hunched over, and two of its large branches extended downward into the ground like arms. The tree's roots were pulled loose from the dirt and snaked backward along the ground behind it.

As Wily neared the tree, he felt his heart jump. There, dangling from a high branch on the Crawlin' Tree's back, was an iron lantern with a crystal dangling from the bottom.

"We need something to light it with," Wily called back to the others, who were hurrying toward him.

As she came to a stop nearby, Odette reached into her pouch and pulled out a tinder stone.

"You know how to use this?" Odette asked as Wily snatched it from her hand.

Wily moved to Roveeka's side. She was huffing from the walk, nearly out of breath.

"I need to borrow Mum." Wily barely got the words out before Roveeka was handing him the slightly curved dagger.

With knife and tinder stone in hand, Wily climbed his way up one of the Crawlin' Tree's outstretched arms to the iron lantern. Up close, he could see that it was covered in elaborate designs similar to the ones inscribed on the floor of the Carrion Tomb's summoning chamber. This was a magic lantern.

He opened the small glass door on the side of it and straightened the wick. It had to glow as brightly as it could. He slid the side of Mum against the rough edge of the tinder stone, creating a flicker of tiny sparks. One of the sparks landed on the wick. At once it lit up with a crackling yellow glow.

As he closed the door, a wave of hope rushed over his body.

"How is anyone going to see that tiny light?" Roveeka asked. "I can barely see it from down here."

"It's a signal lantern," Pryvyd answered. "It is magically connected to other identical lanterns that will begin to glow whenever this one does."

"Now all we have to do is wait," Wily said, scanning the tree line.

"It's almost dark," Odette said from the tree root she was sitting on.

Wily was still perched on the tree branch, his back straight, eyes alert. Many hours had passed since Wily had lit the lantern. The only thing he had spotted, though, was a pair of ghostly chipmunks, scampering through the blackened leaves that littered the ground. No sign of his mother or any other living thing for that matter. But he knew she would come. She had to.

"How much longer do you want to sit here?" Odette said as she tightened the laces of her boot.

"As long as it takes," Wily said, setting his chin.

"Hold on," Odette said, alarmed. "That wasn't part of the deal."

"I'm changing the deal," Wily retorted.

"No, not okay. At night, the ghosts gain strength.

They take on physical form. Think about what those elks did to you when they were weakened by the sunlight."

"You're not going to change my mind," Wily said, determined.

"I don't want a pack of undead gristle hounds tearing me to shreds in the middle of the night," Odette said. "I don't think anybody else wants that to happen to them either."

Odette looked to the others.

"I understand where you are coming from, Wily," Pryvyd said. "But Odette does have a point. I don't want to see any of us get hurt. Including you."

Moshul signed his response. Pryvyd translated.

"Moshul says even the ground is warning us to leave."

"I'm with Wily," Roveeka said, putting her hands on her hips. "We stay until his mother comes."

Odette leaped to her feet, suddenly angry.

"You know what, I'm tired of pretending here," Odette spit out, eyes bright. "Wily's mother is not coming. She was looking for him a decade ago. You know what you do after ten years of someone being missing? You move on. You give up."

"Why are you so mean?" Roveeka asked.

"I'm not mean," Odette said. "I'm realistic. I know how the world works. I haven't been stuck in some dungeon my whole life."

"Well, I think she's going to come," Roveeka countered.

"You've got a lot to learn about life," Odette snapped back.

"I know that I may not be the smartest," Roveeka said to Odette. "But I know what's right. If I had a chance to have a family, I would do anything to find them. You don't know what that's like."

"Oh, but I do," Odette said, her anger giving way to sadness. "My parents were captured by the Infernal King when I was seven. I spent five years trying to rescue them from the prisonaut where they were held. But every plan I had would fail. There were days I thought of giving myself over to the king's gearfolk, just for the chance to be imprisoned with my parents. But I knew that would break their hearts. They wanted more than anything for me to be free."

The words spilled from Odette in a rush as if she had been holding them in for years.

"I should have given up," Odette continued. "But I was stupid. I trained and practiced for years until I could climb anything, even the walls of a prisonaut. When I knew I was ready, in the dead of night I climbed the outer walls of my parents' prisonaut, knocked out the guards patrolling the tower, and snuck my way through the maze of buildings until I found their sleeping barracks. I found out they had died three days earlier, trying to escape."

Odette fell silent.

Nobody knew what to say. Eventually, Roveeka spoke up. "I didn't know," she said quietly with genuine empathy in her voice.

"I'm not looking for anyone's sympathy," Odette said. "I just don't want to waste any more of my life on false hopes."

Suddenly, Righteous pulled its sword from Pryvyd's sheath.

Wily spun away from the argument to see a figure approaching through the trees. It was a long-haired squatling with a pair of lavender wings that hugged her shoulders. In her hand she carried a lantern.

Wily scampered down from the branch he was perched on. As his feet touched the ground, he could better see the squatling approaching. Her face was gently wrinkled and her hair was streaked with wisps of gray. A brown bird with a golden beak sat on her shoulder.

"Why have you lit the signal lantern?" her gravelly voice called out.

"I am looking for my mother," Wily said, the words stiff on his lips.

"And who would you be?" the flightless fairy asked.

"I'm Wily Snare," he said, holding his head high.

"That's not possible," the squatling said as she moved closer.

She studied Wily intently as she approached. The bird on her shoulder seemed to be examining him as well.

"I have the scar to prove it."

Wily rolled up his sleeve to reveal the strange-shaped burn mark on his arm.

She paused as if entranced by the scar. Then: "I thought this day would never come."

"Do you know where my mother is?" Wily asked, expectation welling up within him.

"Your mother, Lumina Arbus, died trying to stop the Infernal King."

Wily felt the whole world drop away. She couldn't possibly have said those words. He refused to believe it. All he needed to do was wake up. He was certain of it. He was dreaming. In the morning, reality would return. He would stir from the bed in the prisonaut's sleeping barracks and he would set off to find the Crawlin' Tree.

Wily hesitantly looked around at the others. Roveeka was about to cry, even if Wily couldn't. Pryvyd and Moshul both hung their heads low. Even Odette looked heartbroken.

After a long moment of silence, Wily spoke again.

"Is my father dead as well?"

The gray-haired squatling looked at Wily.

"No," she said with more sorrow. "He isn't. But I wish he was."

THE SAD TALE OF
LUMINA ARBUS

"**S**it down," the lavender-winged squatling said as she lowered herself to the ground. "I think you deserve to hear the whole story, and it is not a short one."

Wily took a seat on one of the arms of the Crawlin' Tree between Odette and Pryvyd. Roveeka sat cross-legged on the forest floor next to the lady.

"My name is Epenya Veldt, and I knew your mother since the day she was born. We were both members of the nomadic tribe of humans, elves, and squatlings known as the Roamabout. We lived in the wild forests and fields and mountains. Like all children of our tribe, your mother, Lumina, was taught to be a beast queller, learning to tame and train creatures that most people would find terrifying.

"On the day after her twenty-fifth birthday, while traveling through the woods near Trumpet Pass, she stumbled upon a young man cornered by a quill grizzler. She quelled the wild animal and rescued the man, only to discover that he was Kestrel, the youngest prince of the Gromanov family. He had been out on an expedition to find parts for his latest invention, a mechanical man he called a gearfolk. From then on, they met in the woods in secret to talk about their dreams for the kingdom. Despite, or perhaps because of, their very different upbringings, they fell in love. They were wed before the next solstice. It was only after their wedding that Kestrel began to change into the cruel king he would become."

Wily was suddenly sitting up very straight. *My mother was married to Kestrel Gromanov?* He wondered how long that had lasted before she had met his father.

"Kestrel seized control of the throne from his father," Epenya said, "and began spreading his army of gearfolk across the land. Your mother tried to stop him but, over the next year, Lumina learned a difficult lesson: people are not as easy to quell as dragons and giant spiders. She wanted to help Kestrel return to himself—to the kind, benevolent man she had met in the woods . . . but the more she tried, the more he resisted. Kestrel had lessons to learn as well. He thought that Lumina would be a loyal and unquestioning follower of his every command, just like his machines. How very wrong he was. Both your father and mother understood very little about relationships."

Something inside Wily stilled at the word *father*.

"But despite their difficulties, you were already on the way. On the first anniversary of their wedding, Lumina gave birth to you. Your father named you after the author of his favorite book. Your mother loved you dearly. . . . For a brief while, you brought happiness to them both and made their differences wash away.

"Then one day when you father was supposed to be caring for you, he became distracted by his latest invention, a mechanical suit of armor. You tried to touch it while it was still in the flames. That's how you got the burn on your arm."

In a daze, Wily pulled up his sleeve and looked at the pattern of the cracked moon branded into his skin. What had been a symbol of hope not an hour before had transformed into a traitorous symbol of a terrible lineage.

"When your mother learned of what had happened,"

Epenya continued, "she threatened to leave with you. Kestrel flew into a rage. The next day when Lumina came to your crib, she found you missing. Kestrel had hidden you away. He told her that she would not be allowed to see you until she could be trusted. Lumina knew that no matter how subservient she playacted, he would never trust her again. She snuck away in the middle of the night.

"Kestrel's rage only grew. His hatred of anything he couldn't control was now complete. He surrounded himself with more and more of his machines and took on a new name."

"The Infernal King," Wily said with a heavy heart.

"Yes, Wily," said Epenya. "The Infernal King is your father."

It felt like his body was going to melt, rolling down the sides of the Crawlin' Tree branch and soaking into the hard dark earth.

"What happened to my mother?" Wily asked, his voice weak.

"Lumina was not prepared to give up on you," Epenya said calmly. "She contacted the best bounty hunters in all the land and, without revealing her true identity, gave them very clear instructions. If a boy with a scar shaped like a cracked moon is ever found, light the lantern in the Crawlin' Tree. Your mother herself searched for many years but never found you.

"Years later, when the Infernal King released the first prisonaut upon the land, your mother knew she had to confront him. She went to the fortress to tell him to stop his cruelty and end the madness. She never returned. Now every year on the high moon, we mourn her death."

Epenya took a long, soft breath before falling silent.

Wily got to his feet and walked away. He wasn't sure where he was going, but he needed to think without all his companion's eyes burrowing into his skin.

He found a rock wedged between two dead trees and collapsed on top of it.

It was all too much to even process. His mother was dead. His father was the worst person in the Above. He was the heir to a kingdom he barely knew.

He felt a hand on his shoulder. He turned to see Roveeka standing behind him.

"I know your family isn't what you were hoping for," Roveeka said quietly, "but I'll always be your sister."

Wily reached up and took her hand between his and leaned his entire weight against her body. He squeezed her arm tightly.

"I'm so glad you're with me," Wily said. "I never could have done this alone."

"We're the strongest kind of family, because we chose each other."

Roveeka put a gentle hand on his head.

"If there is a path into the darkest dungeon," Roveeka said, "there's always a way out, too."

Wily thought about her words.

After a period of stillness, he stood up with new direction.

He walked back to the group, who had barely moved since he'd left.

"I'm ready to go to Ratgull Harbor," Wily said.

"I think that's a good decision," Pryvyd said.

Moshul signed to the others.

"Moshul thinks so, too," Pryvyd translated.

The moss golem continued signing.

"He also thinks we are being watched."

"It's the ghosts of the forest waking," Epenya said. "They won't harm me, but they're not so kind to strangers."

Wily heard the burned leaves rustling behind him. He turned quickly, and for a moment, thought he saw a pair of yellow eyes staring back at him from inside a rotted log.

Looking closer, though, nothing was there.

"If we leave now," Pryvyd said, "we can still make it out of the Twighast before dark."

Odette was still sitting quietly on the Crawlin' Tree. She hadn't said a word, which wasn't like her at all.

Wily walked over to Epenya.

"Thank you for telling me the truth," Wily said.

"I know it's not the truth you wanted to hear," Epenya said as she took his hands in hers. "But know you always have a place with the Roamabouts. We would welcome you with open arms."

"I need to get as far away from Panthasos as I can," Wily replied, "away from the Infernal King." He couldn't bring himself to say *father*.

Wily took one last look at the lantern glowing on the back of the Crawlin' Tree and started back through the trees.

THE TRIP OUT of the Twighast was easier than the journey in, as they only needed to follow the path of broken branches and golem footprints. The mood, though, was dismal. Wily could tell that everyone (but Roveeka) was too uncomfortable to speak to him. Only occasionally would anyone even glance in his direction and, if they did, they quickly turned away before making eye contact.

As the putrid stench of the swamp ahead began to waft through the air, Wily decided to break the silence.

"I know what you're thinking," Wily announced. "And I get why all of you can barely look at me. I'm the son of a monster. My father has ruined all of your lives."

"We know it's not your fault," Pryvyd said.

"But it is," Wily said. "That's the truth. If I had never been born and reached into the flames, Kestrel Gromanov would not have gotten into a giant fight with my mother. She would have never left him. And he wouldn't have become so angry that he turned into the Infernal King."

"You can't think that way," Pryvyd said.

"Why shouldn't I?" Wily spit back. "If it wasn't for me, you'd still have your arm. And Odette would still have her family."

"But we wouldn't all be together," Roveeka said.

"That's right, because you'd all be happy," Wily said. "And I wouldn't be here. Which would be better for the whole world. I thought I didn't belong in the tomb, and now I know that I don't belong out here either."

"Don't say those things," Odette said, getting angry.

"I'm just laying out the facts," Wily said.

"Well, I don't want to hear them," Odette said as she sped up her pace.

They made it out of the haunted forest with little time to spare. The sun had already dipped below the mountains, and only the pink clouds were still illuminating the limestone-gray sky. A swarm of mosquitoes and weltwings welcomed them back to the murk of the swamp.

"I think I can see the outline of the fallen prisonaut's high tower in the distance," Roveeka said.

Wily could barely make out the object at which she was now pointing. Her hobgoblet eyes again had adjusted to the enveloping darkness faster than his.

They continued to move in the direction of the silhouette ahead. After another thousand paces, everyone else could see what Wily's hobgoblet half sister had already spied. The prisonaut was just a short distance away.

"I told you that was the prisonaut," Roveeka said, trying her best to be cheerful.

"No one doubted you," Odette said, smacking a fat weltwing on the back of her neck.

"AGH!" Pryvyd screamed. And it wasn't a little scream that you might make from the bite of a hungry weltwing. Before Wily could spin around, he heard the sound of Pryvyd's armor hitting the ground hard.

Wily turned to spot Pryvyd on his stomach, a giant claw clamped down on his leg, squeezing so tightly it was bending the metal armor around the knight's thigh.

Just beyond, the two heads of a baby crab dragon were peeking out of its mud hole. The horse-size magical crustacean was the same murky gray as the mud it was partially submerged in. Crab dragons' shells only developed color when they were older and strong enough to defend themselves against larger predators.

"Get this thing off me!" Pryvyd called out.

Righteous was first to respond to his cry. It flew over with sword in hand and hit the blade against the tough exoskeleton of the claw repeatedly.

"That's only going to make her squeeze tighter!" Wily shouted.

Moshul reached down and grabbed the crab dragon by the claw. He tried to pry it apart to free Pryvyd, but was having no greater success than the floating arm.

Odette plucked an exploding mushroom off Moshul's back and prepared to throw it.

"Don't hurt her," Wily yelled. "She's just a baby. She's playing."

"This is not a fun game for me," Pryvyd said.

"We can't let her just crack Pryvyd's leg off," Odette yelled back. "This baby doesn't know her own strength."

The baby crab dragon made a playful click before lifting Pryvyd up and smacking him against the ground again.

"Crab dragons are just animals," Wily said. "Let me try communicating with her."

Odette lowered the mushroom hesitantly. Moshul and Righteous backed away. The crab dragon shook Pryvyd like a gristle puppy tussling a chew toy.

"Do something!" Pryvyd shouted.

Wily spread his arms out as wide as he could and bent down so his belly was nearly touching the ground. Then he pressed the front of his tongue to the roof of his mouth. He let air slide out from his lips as he made clicking sounds.

"Click-click-CLICK-click-CLICK-CLICK," Wily said in his best Mandible. (The rough translation was "Don't eat that man. It would be a very big mistake.")

The baby crab dragon was surprised that a person was speaking her language.

"Why not?" one of the two crab-dragon heads clicked back, knocking her mandibles together rapidly. "I've almost cracked the meat out of the shell."

The crab dragon squeezed down harder on Pryvyd's leg, fracturing the bronze armor.

"He's spoiled and will give you indigestion," Wily urgently responded back in a chain of clicks.

The crab dragon paused. The two heads looked at each other as if considering what to do next.

Then the dragon slowly released its grip. Pryvyd seized the moment, pulling his leg free from the claw. He hobbled past Wily, who still had his arms outstretched.

"You don't want to eat any of us," Wily explained in Mandible. "We all taste worse than cave rats."

The baby crab dragon began taking steps in reverse, backing toward its mud hole. Before the giant crustacean disappeared into the darkness, it clicked one last message.

"I believe you," one crab-dragon head said.

"But my older sisters and brothers won't," finished the other head.

Wily's face went pale when he heard those final clicks.

He turned around to see a clatter of six full-size crab dragons, each triple the size of Moshul and sporting bright yellow-and-orange spots on their shells, emerging from the muddy earth. All twelve heads looked viciously at the group of wanderers who were trespassing through their territory. They snapped their claws menacingly in the air.

Pryvyd, Righteous, Odette, Moshul, Roveeka, and Wily tightened into a circle, pressing their bodies close together as the crab dragons moved in on them.

"Do that clicking thing again," Odette said in a panic.

Wily didn't even get out one click before the largest of the crab dragons began rapidly gnashing its spiked mandibles.

"We're going to eat all of you," the large crab dragon clicked menacingly, its two heads alternating every other click. "Except the pile of mud. We're just going to break it into little pieces for fun."

"And you won't be changing our minds," clicked a crab dragon with a chink in its shell.

"I'm not sure there is anything I can click to get us out of this one," Wily said to his friends gravely.

"Then we'll fight," Pryvyd said, gripping his spiked shield tight in his hand.

Righteous swung his sword bravely.

"We got this," Odette said confidently.

"Where should I hit them?" Roveeka asked, pulling Mum and Pops from her waistband.

A crab dragon with black spots covering its shell scampered forward, reaching its claw out for Odette. She was way too fast for him, though, and backflipped onto Moshul's shoulder.

"Now!" she screamed.

Moshul swung a massive punch with his right arm at one of the charging crab dragon's heads.

The mighty fist made contact with the beast's head—

—and did nothing. The crab dragon barely seemed to have noticed the attack.

"On the other hand," Odette said, "maybe you want to try that clicking thing again."

The crab dragons were closing in around Wily and the others. Drool dripped from the corners of the dragons' mouths, evaporating into steam as it hit the wet earth.

The crab dragon with the chink in its shell stretched a claw toward Wily's unprotected torso.

BANG-CLACK-BANG.

The sound was coming from behind the largest of the crab dragons.

BANG-CLACK-BANG.

A figure dressed in a black cloak held two large wooden sticks and was smashing them together over and over. The face of the stranger was completely obscured by scarves.

"The Scarf," Odette breathed in awe.

One of the dragons thrust his head out to bite the Scarf. Yet the Scarf showed no fear.

BANG-CLACK-BANG.

The attacking crab dragon froze in place as if hypnotized. The Scarf kept banging the sticks, moving closer and closer to the beast, unafraid of its teeth or man-dibles. The crustacean lowered its claws and bowed its heads submissively.

The Scarf raised both sticks overhead and showed them to the other crab dragons. After another loud BANG, the shelled creatures skittered backward, van-ishing into the murk and tall reeds.

"Thank you for your assistance," Pryvyd said aloud.

The Scarf did not respond. Instead, the stranger reached beneath the long black robe and pulled out a small lantern. Wily recognized it. It looked identical to the lantern from the Crawlin' Tree.

The Scarf walked swiftly, straight toward the group. And, with every step, pulled off one of the many colored scarves, letting each fall to the ground.

Yellow. Blue. Green. Silver. Purple.

Beneath the scarves, Wily could see the face of a wise, confident woman. The face looked so familiar . . . familiar because it resembled his own.

"Wily," the woman said. "My boy."

18

A TURN AT THE BEND

"I couldn't tell anyone," Lumina said after she had released her long-lost son from a tight embrace. "Not even the Roamabouts. It was for everyone's safety. If your father knew what I was doing . . ."

Lumina reached out and touched Wily's cheek. He instinctively pushed his face into her palm, letting her smooth fingertips cradle his ear.

"I searched all of Panthasos for you," Lumina said.

Wily's mother pulled a metal tube from her pocket. She popped one of the caps off and pulled out a piece of parchment. She unrolled it, revealing a map of Panthasos with a thousand tiny *x* marks all over it.

"Where did he hide you?"

"I was the trapsmith of Carrion Tomb," Wily answered.

"How clever of your father," Lumina said. "He was able to train you while keeping you captured. I should have looked there. I'm so sorry."

Lumina took a quill pen out of her pouch and placed a small *w* over the spot where the entrance to Carrion Tomb was located.

"You'll never have to search for me again," Wily said with a wide smile.

Yet no smile could ever be wide enough to capture what he was feeling right now. It was as if a thousand moments of happiness had just broken free from their chains and been set loose in his heart.

Just then, from a patch of reeds, Wily heard a rustling. He had almost forgotten he was standing in the middle of a swamp. As soon as he had wrapped his arms around his mother, it was as if his surroundings had vanished. Only now did he even realize that his companions were standing around him, smiling.

Wily heard the rustle again and saw a pair of yellow eyes staring out from within. The same ones he had seen in the hollow log back in the Twighast. A second pair of eyes stared out, too.

"Come on out and meet my son," Lumina beckoned to the tall grass.

Out into the moonlight bounded two skinny furred creatures. Their coats were as black as a torchless cave, and they wore tiny belts with tools on them. One of them had a splash of white on his belly, and the other was missing most of her tail. Wily had seen them once before, destroying the snagglecarts and gearfolk in Vale Village.

"Are these rats yours?" Wily asked.

"They're ferrets," Lumina answered, "and they don't belong to anyone. But they do join me on my missions."

The one with the missing tail crawled up Wily's leg and took a seat on his knee. The other curled up into Lumina's lap.

"That's Impish," she said, pointing to the one who was snooping in Wily's pockets. "She likes taking things that don't belong to her. And breaking stuff."

"Like gearfolk?" Wily asked.

"Exactly," Lumina replied. "And this is Gremlin. He dismantled four snagglecarts all by himself. His favorite hobby is making things explode." She laughed softly.

Wily eyed the ferret now sleeping in her lap. He wondered how this cute ball of fur could do anything of the sort. If he had not borne witness to their handiwork, it would have seemed most impossible.

"Impish!" Lumina scolded. "Put that back."

Impish had pulled out the puzzle box from Wily's side satchel and was turning it about in her tiny clawed paws.

"Actually," Wily said, "it doesn't belong to me."

Wily took the box from Impish.

"You can have it," Wily said to Odette. "I don't need it anymore."

Wily flipped the box over and used his nail to find a secret lever. He pulled it free while twisting the top in three concentric circles. A dozen more twists and secret button presses and the box popped open to reveal the Sun Stone.

"That was all I needed to do? I could have figured that out," Odette joked.

"A Sun Stone?" Lumina said, surprised, peering inside. "Your father has been looking for another. He has one that powers the Infernal Fortress. Another he fractured, putting slivers of it into the prisonauts and snagglecarts. Who knows what he would do with a third?"

Wily took a tiny screwdriver from his trapsmith belt and recalibrated the cogs and gears of the puzzle box with a few quick twists. Then he handed the box to Odette.

"You have so much of both your father and me in

you," Lumina said as she watched Wily twirl the screw-driver in his hand, before he slid it back into his tool belt. "The way you quelled that crab dragon. And how good you are with machines."

"I hope that's the only thing I have in common with my father," Wily said.

"That," Lumina said, "and his eyes. He did have pretty eyes."

"And he's a cruel madman," Odette added. "Don't forget about that."

"I know all too well," Lumina said, "which is why I spent the last ten years trying to right the wrongs he's committed. I've even tried breaking into the Infernal Fortress in an attempt to stop him once and for all, but he has rigged the entire palace with traps that are far beyond even my ability to disable. I barely made it out with my life."

Lumina then turned to her son.

"But my most important mission was trying to find you."

Wily felt as if his heart were so full it might burst.

"Mom," Wily said, letting the wonderful word roll off his tongue, "we're going to the Salt Isles. Far away from Panthasos, where my father can't hurt us. Will you come with me?"

Am I asking too much? She has spent the last dozen years as the Scarf, and I know there are many more important—

"Wily," Lumina said, "it's going to be a very long time before you can get rid of me."

She grabbed him and pulled him in close once more. Wily didn't know if it was the smell of her hair or the way her fingers rested on the back of his neck, but he had the strangest feeling that everything was going to be all right from this day forth.

oᴼo

AFTER SPENDING THE night in the fallen prisonaut, the group of nine followed the edge of the lake through the rest of the swamp. They passed the discarded junk barge they had used to flee from the Floating City and continued to the west.

"At Buckswallow Bend," Odette said, with her typical morning exuberance, "we should be able to purchase horses. It's a great little elfin village."

Then she added her all-too-common refrain.

"It's not far from here."

Wily gave Odette a look.

"I know I say that a lot, but it's true," Odette insisted. "Buckswallow is just over the next hill. Or so."

It didn't matter to Wily how far away Buckswallow

was (or any other town for that matter). He was walking with his mother. The colorful scarves around her neck fluttered with every step. It almost seemed as if she were being followed by an ever-changing sunset. He couldn't imagine anyone more lovely in the whole world.

Lumina caught Wily staring and gave him a tender wink. She pressed her lips together and whistled warmly. From a nearby patch of flowers, a tremble of butterflies winged upward and swirled around Lumina and Wily.

"You've got to teach me how to do that," Wily exclaimed.

"And give away all my secrets?" Lumina countered with a raised eyebrow. "I am the Scarf, you know. I need to keep a little air of mystery."

With another whistle, the butterflies all landed on Wily's shoulders. Looking at the delicate wings, Wily wondered how he had been so terrified of these beautiful creatures only a few days before.

The group continued to the top of the next rise. The wind had bellowed strongly the night before and any trace of cloud or haze had been blown away. The view in every direction was magnificent. There were many reasons to leave Panthasos (all of which having to do with the Infernal King), but it was impossible to ignore the wonders that it held.

"See, what did I tell you?" Odette said, pointing out a small town nestled in the bend of a river. "Wait until you try the spiced hot chocolate in Balbers's Flavor Shop."

Then, with an even bouncier than usual bounce in her step, she started down the rise.

"I can't tell what I like less," Pryvyd said, "her nasty streak in the evening or that?"

Moshul pointed ahead to Odette doing a cartwheel.

"Yeah, I agree," Pryvyd said to Moshul with a smirk. "That."

Odette, completely unaware that she was being talked about, did a tumble into a split.

Pryvyd, Moshul, Roveeka, and Wily all shared a chuckle.

"Hurry up," Odette called over her shoulder as she rushed ahead.

Halfway to Buckswallow, Odette froze in her tracks.

Wily, catching up, could see something horrible had befallen the town. Many of the cottages had been burned and the others toppled. The fishing boats along the river had been broken, scraps of wood littering the shore. The only remaining structure left untouched was the stone bridge.

"There truly is no safe place left in Panthasos," Odette said sadly.

Odette let strands of her blue hair fall in front of her face. Through them, Wily could see that Odette's eyes were welling with tears. Before he could approach her, she pushed ahead.

As they got closer, it came as little surprise that there were no more elves in Buckswallow. The animals were gone, too.

Odette stopped before a charred structure, brushing the hair away from her now-dry eyes. The stone arch-way of the door still stood, but the wooden walls and roof were nothing but ash. Beyond the doorway, tables and chairs still waited for customers who would never come again.

She walked into what was left of the dining establishment and took a seat at one of the tables.

"I sat here with my father once," Odette said quietly. "We each got a hot chocolate and more cookies than we could eat."

"What's a cookie?" Roveeka asked as she came up beside the table.

Wily was wondering the same thing, but he thought it wasn't the appropriate time to ask such a trivial question.

Suddenly, Roveeka tore Mum and Pops out of her

waistband. She held the sharp tip of Mum between her fingers, prepared to throw it at the cupboard.

"This could be an ambush," Roveeka warned.

Wily spied, through the slightly ajar door, a small person tucked inside. The person looked scared, not dangerous.

"Come out so we can see you," Wily said to the hidden figure.

The door creaked open and a small elf girl emerged, followed by her even smaller brother.

Lumina approached the children slowly.

"Where are your parents?" Lumina asked gently.

Her voice was so calm and reassuring that the panic on their faces quickly disappeared. It was hard to believe that this was the same woman who had destroyed a hundred snagglecarts.

"The gearfolk took them," the girl said. "They took all the grown-ups."

"We'll take you to the next town," Pryvyd said, "where you'll be cared for."

"We're waiting for them to come back," the little elf boy said.

"No," Lumina said sweetly. "It's not safe here."

Pryvyd reached out a gentle hand, but the elf

snatched her brother by the arm and sprinted for the fireplace. They pressed a secret lever in the soot and a trapdoor opened beneath them. The two elves slid into the darkness below. By the time Wily and the others got to the fireplace, the trapdoor had closed.

"There must be elf tunnels beneath the village," Odette said. "It could take us days to find them under there."

"Their parents aren't coming back, are they?" Roveeka asked.

"Once someone goes into the prisonaut," Odette answered, "they never come out."

Lumina nodded in agreement.

The thought made Wily bristle. He hated the idea of children being torn from their parents. He thought back on the two girls who were nearly separated from their mother by the gearfolk in Vale Village and the younger girl's tears. He knew what that felt like. It was horrible. He couldn't bear to think of other children separated from the people that they cared about, especially now that he knew the joy of having his own mother in his life.

"It doesn't have to be that way," Wily said, determined.

"Yes, it does," Odette said. "Even if we broke into the prisonaut, it would be too difficult to find the elves' parents and get them out."

"I'm not talking about freeing one set of parents," Wily said. "I'm saying we free everyone."

Pryvyd nearly stumbled back into Moshul. "And how would that happen?" Pryvyd asked, genuinely baffled by the suggestion.

"We break into the Infernal Fortress and grovblunder the king," Wily said.

Roveeka and Righteous moved in closer, listening intently. Odette began shaking her head as if that were the most ridiculous suggestion she'd ever heard.

"That's impossible," Odette said.

"Wily," Lumina explained, "I've already tried that. Many times."

"But not with me," Wily said. "Not with us."

None of them looked convinced. Except for Righteous. The arm had already moved to Wily's side and was holding its fist aloft in a gesture of support.

"I know traps," Wily said. "I can get us through. I'll need all your help, of course. But I'm certain this is what we are meant to do."

It took a moment for the others to realize just how serious Wily was.

"This is the reason I was brought out of the tomb," Wily said, his heart beating with the thrill of certainty. "Not to run away to the Salt Isles. But to face my father and set things right. Back in the tomb, I always wished the books on my shelf told stories of families being reunited. I never thought my story could end that way. So now that it has, how could I leave Panthasos when I can help other people's stories come true, too?"

"For a kid who spent his whole life in a cave, you know an awful lot about the world," his mother said, beaming at him with pride. She rolled up her sleeves to reveal a pair of very strong biceps. "I'll help in any way I can. With or without my scarves."

Wily looked to his friends hopefully.

"I may still have some knight left in me," Pryvyd said. "I'm with you, Wily."

Pryvyd stepped forward. Righteous pumped his fist excitedly and took its place next to Pryvyd's shoulder.

Moshul signaled to Wily. He wasn't sure what the moss golem had said, but a moment later, the golem moved to Wily's side.

"Are you going to hold the Sun Stone hostage again?" Odette asked.

"No," Wily said. "This decision you get to make on your own."

Odette crossed her arms, considering.

"The Salt Isles sound boring, anyway," Odette said with a smile. "And I hate boring."

"When we asked the Oracle of Oak for the trapsmith to help us on our mission," Pryvyd said, "I thought the mission was raiding dungeons. Maybe this is the mission we were meant to go on all along."

"Then we leave for the Infernal Fortress now," Wily said. "I'm sure it's 'not far from here.'"

"Actually," Odette said, "it's about a week's walk."

"There's no time to lose," Wily said. "Let's go."

They were all about to leave when Roveeka cleared her throat.

"I know everybody just assumes I'm coming along," Roveeka said aloud, "but no one ever asked what I think."

"You're right, sis," Wily said apologetically. "What do you think?"

Roveeka pondered a moment, then came to her conclusion.

"It's a great idea. Let's do it!"

19

NEVER-SCAPE

During the six-day journey from Buckswallow, Lumina had told Wily many stories about the grand majesty of the royal palace that had once belonged to his grandparents. She described the singing sculptures in the enchanted garden and the master map in the study that magically changed with every new bridge built, road paved, or tree planted. She described the dining hall with a glass floor that looked down upon the kitchen where the food was being prepared. She explained how on every full moon the courtyard was filled with guests from every corner of Panthasos, squatlings and slither trolls alike. And she told him of how his father had slowly corroded all of it.

Staring out at the Infernal Fortress now, it was hard for Wily to imagine that it had ever been the place that she described. The once-gleaming white walls were stained black with dripping tar and covered with spinning blades that constantly moved along hidden tracks in the stone. The orchards outside the palace were no longer a bounty of fruit, but instead a junkyard of scrapped and damaged snagglecarts. And the flag that fluttered from the highest tower bore the three-horned helmet of the Infernal King.

"See there," Lumina said, pointing to a cluster of rocks near the jet-black moat. "Between the rocks is a secret door that leads into the fortress's dungeon."

"How do you know?" Pryvyd asked.

"Because it's the same one I used to escape twelve years ago," Lumina said, narrowing her eyes in memory. "More than once I've tried sneaking back in, but Kestrel's filled it with traps."

Lumina stepped away from the overlook and began stretching her legs and arms. She was extremely flexible, which came as little surprise, considering how often she was jumping down from buildings.

Roveeka sat next to Moshul, who had Impish and Gremlin foraging for grubs on his back. Her stomach grumbled noisily.

"Can I eat this one?" Roveeka asked the moss golem as she pulled a plump maroon root out of his foot.

"Not unless you want to start a fire in your belly," Odette said. "An actual fire."

Roveeka carefully put the root down. She grabbed a salted lizard leg from her snacking pouch and ate that instead.

While the others filled their bellies, Wily kept staring at the fortress, doubt wheedling him. He had led them all here with the promise that he'd be able to get them through. *What if I can't?*

"If it was easy," Pryvyd said, as he came up alongside Wily, "it would have already been done. You'll try your best. That's all anyone can ever do."

Wily imagined the ship sailing from Ratgull Harbor. They could have all been on their way to the Salt Isles by now.

"I think it is time," Pryvyd called to the others.

The group left their cover and moved swiftly across the lifeless plain toward the Infernal Fortress. As they hurried to the cluster of rocks near the moat, Wily glanced up at the high tower. He wondered if his father was watching them from above.

Between the rocks was the entrance to a tunnel. The group did not have to venture far inside before they came to a steel door. It was thicker than a turtle-dragon shell, and it glowed brightly with a powerful enchantment. It was also wide open.

"What a stroke of luck," Odette said as she stepped through the open door.

"No," Lumina said, shaking her head emphatically. "This is misfortune. He left the door open on purpose. He must have some new trap he wants to test."

"Or it was an accident," Odette countered.

Lumina tried to keep herself from dismissing Odette too callously.

"Kestrel doesn't make mistakes like this," Lumina explained calmly. "We should turn back."

"He's playing games with us," Wily said, "trying to keep us off-balance. I would use the same trick back in the tomb. Keep the invaders paranoid. We can't fall for it."

Wily took the lead. He passed through the enchanted door and into a long dark tunnel that sloped down. The ground soon became slick with moisture.

"We must be going under the moat," Odette said as she pointed to the ceiling.

Thick drops of black water seeped from the cracks above, giving the impression that the entire tunnel could flood at any moment.

Squish.

Wily lifted his foot. He bent down and scooped up a translucent glob of ooze off the ground.

"We're not alone in here," Wily said.

Behind them, he heard the enchanted door slam shut.

"This is amoebolith slime," Wily continued.

"Is that what you call . . . *that*?" Odette said, looking ahead.

Wily gazed up to see a translucent amoebolith heading their way. It filled the entire passage with its massive gelatinous body. Dozens of arrows and a pair of swords were suspended in the giant single-celled beast's clear, gooey form, along with a wide assortment of bones and suits of armor.

"Stay back," Roveeka said to the others. "Being slowly digested by a giant blob is a very unpleasant way to die."

The group looked terrified. All except Wily. He had a big grin on his face.

"Wily," Lumina asked, very confused, "why are you smiling?"

"Because this just might be easier than I thought," Wily replied. "Roveeka, give me your snacking bag."

Wily snagged the small burlap sack hanging from Roveeka's shoulder. He reached into the snacking bag and pulled out the lizard leg Roveeka had been munching on.

"I don't think a tiny lizard leg is going to satisfy the hunger of a giant blob," Odette said in a panic.

Wily tossed the lizard leg over his shoulder. Then he tipped the bag into his hand. A fistful of course salt grains came pouring out.

The amoebolith, sensing the vibrations of Odette's rapidly beating heart, formed a bubbling arm from its belly goo and stretched it toward her. Odette dodged backward and escaped with only her arm getting drenched in slime.

"That's disgusting," Odette said, shaking her arm off.

Before the amoebolith attempted to engulf her again, Wily leaned down and sprinkled a line of salt across the hall from one wall to the other. He had only just finished when the giant blob surged toward Odette.

The amoebolith's ever-changing body touched the line of salt and immediately recoiled. The portion of the blob's outer layer that had made contact with the grains sizzled. The amoebolith tried to get around the salt, but couldn't find a way. It attempted to climb the wall, but the swords and armor floating inside the blob's body made it too heavy. After a few tense moments, the amoebolith reversed course and headed back toward the pit it had crawled out of, leaving a trail of bubbling jelly in its wake.

"Let's keep moving," Wily said with a cocksure grin.

The long tunnel led them into the castle's wine cellar. The racks were all empty except for thick cobwebs. The light from the nearby staircase cast the room in a soft glow.

Then Wily noticed something that alarmed him. There was no dust on the floor.

But there was a pressure plate.

And Odette was about to step on it.

"Odette!" Wily yelled. "Stop moving!"

He didn't warn her fast enough, though. Her foot pressed down on the pressure plate.

As soon as she did, two halves of a cage came speeding out of the walls. Odette tried to jump out of the way, but the cages were on wheels and moved so quickly that the side of one of the cages struck her in the head. She fell to the floor unconscious as the two cages snapped closed around her and Pryvyd, Lumina, Moshul, Righteous, Wily, Gremlin, and Impish. Only Roveeka, who had been lagging behind, was still free.

Then before Wily could even get a word out, the floor beneath the cage opened up. The cage plunged into the trapdoor and submerged into ankle-high water.

Waist-high water.

The underground compartment was rapidly filling up with water, and there was nowhere to go.

Wily recognized this trap. It was his Wake-No-More. Only it had been changed from putting the victims to sleep with gas to drowning them.

Lumina was already trying to pull the bars apart, her muscles straining against the steel. Righteous was just a hair too big to squeeze through, but that wasn't stopping the arm from trying.

"How do we get out?" Pryvyd said.

"We can't," Wily said. "It's a never-scape. And I made it."

But how did the Infernal King get his hands on the design?

Pryvyd scooped the unconscious Odette from the ground to keep her head from going underwater.

The water was now up to Wily's chest.

"Wily, what should I do?" Roveeka asked from above.

Wily had already forgotten that his half sister was not captured in the never-scape.

"I'm thinking," Wily said. "We need to get the cage out of the water. Fast."

Wily looked up and saw a chandelier hanging just above the trapdoor. Then he spied a coil of old rope near the wine racks.

"I got it!" Wily shouted. "A pulley!"

Just then the water rose above his mouth and the top of the cage. He couldn't speak anymore. Wily and his mother and Pryvyd and Odette were all going to drown.

Roveeka looked panicked.

"A pulley?" Roveeka asked.

All Wily could do was nod. He recalled the failed lessons in the tomb. The pictures and diagrams he had drawn for her. None of them ever seemed to help her understand. He wished that a complicated math equation could get them out of this trap. Or that her incredible knowledge of rocks could save the day. But, right now, all they needed was a pulley.

"Remember," the hobgoblet said to herself. "Remember how a pulley works."

A faint flicker of memory crossed her face.

And she sprung into action. She ran to the rope on the floor and scooped it up. She took one end and tied it to the top of the cage.

Now completely submerged, Wily's chest was tightening. He needed to breathe again. He didn't have much more time.

Roveeka was moving fast. She took the coil of rope and, with a heave, threw it over the metal frame of the chandelier.

Wily was starting to see stars.

The other end of the rope dropped into the cage underwater.

Moshul grabbed the rope and started pulling.

The stars in Wily's field of vision were getting brighter as he grew more light-headed.

Using the pulley, the moss golem pulled the cage out of the water.

Wily took in a giant lungful of air. They were still alive.

"You did it," Wily called out to Roveeka.

She beamed with pride.

Lumina and Moshul together were able to pull the cage apart with much prying. The group exited the never-scape. Pryvyd and Righteous held Odette aloft.

"She's still alive," Pryvyd said. "But it may take some time for her to wake up."

Wily looked at the staircase ahead, then back at Odette.

"We have to go back," Wily said sadly. "We haven't even made it out of the basement and Odette nearly died. This is too much, even for a trapsmith."

No one argued. They turned back for the tunnel that went under the moat.

20

WINGS OF GEARS

Odette was breathing, but only barely. With the fortress looming up behind them, Righteous and Pryvyd laid Odette down on the ground.

"Your father will send out his army of gearfolk soon," Lumina said with a crackle of anger.

"We should get as far away as we can before they come," Pryvyd added.

"Even with all my trapsmithing," Wily said, "I wasn't able to get us through two rooms of the fortress."

"We'll build an army," Pryvyd said. "If all of Panthasos stands together, even the Infernal King will fall."

Odette suddenly began to cough up water. Wily ran to her side as she gasped for air.

"Odette," Wily begged, "are you okay?"

The elf opened her eyes as she coughed up another lungful of water. She looked alarmed.

"Why are we outside again?" she stammered hoarsely.

"We'll try again another day," Wily said. "I'm just glad you're alive."

Odette sat completely up, taking long breaths to regain her senses.

"If it wasn't for Roveeka," Pryvyd said, "we'd all be dead."

Odette turned to the hobgoblet, her face serious.

"I misjudged you from the first time we met," Odette said. "Will you accept my apology?"

"I'll have to think about it," Roveeka said with a smile. She paused for a beat, then added, "Absolutely."

Odette nodded to her and turned back to the fortress. Her face grew angry.

"To think the Infernal King is just sitting up in his high tower," Odette said, "laughing at us. If I could get my hands on him . . ."

"We'll find a way," Pryvyd said. "Sometime soon."

"Roveeka," Odette continued, "you think you could

throw Mum or Pops up ten stories and knock him hard in the helmet?"

"I wish," Roveeka responded. "Only the birks can get that high."

"Birds," Pryvyd corrected.

"Right," Roveeka said, correcting herself. "Birds. I always forget what they're called."

Wily looked up at the tower.

"Maybe we could get up there."

"You mean climb up the outside?" Lumina asked. "It won't be easy. He's rigged it with moving blades and booby traps just like inside."

"Odette is an amazing climber," Roveeka said with a smile.

"I'm not saying we climb," Wily continued. "What if we could fly?"

"There's no bird strong enough to carry us," Pryvyd said.

"I'm going to build us one."

THE FOUR GEARFOLK standing guard around the snagglecarts never even saw the rust fairy that came to warn them about the trespassers. The blunt end of Mum hit the fairy in the back of the head, knocking her out of the sky.

What the gearfolk did see were a dozen pink onions hit the ground at their feet, exploding into a thick fog of spores and stench.

"Where did that come from?" one of the gearfolk screeched as it tried to roll clear from the haze.

It didn't make it far. Lumina jumped onto its back and popped its helmet off. When a second gearfolk rolled toward the first to lend a hand and a hook stick, Odette vaulted herself onto its back. She grabbed the helmet and tried to tug it off.

"Twist first," Lumina said, pulling the rust-fairy cage from her gearfolk. "Tug after."

"Thanks," Odette said as she wrenched the head off the mechanical man she was standing on.

"Do that a thousand times and you'll have arms stronger than a slither troll's," Lumina called to Odette.

Wily slid down from his perch on Moshul's back as Pryvyd and Righteous handled the other two gearfolk guards. Wily pulled out his screwdriver and got to work breaking apart the snagglecart.

"Can I help?" Roveeka asked, running up beside Wily.

Wily tossed her his extra screwdriver.

"I need to get the whole top part of the cage off the base," Wily said. "It must have a thousand screws. So every hand counts."

Moshul reached down and grabbed the top of the snagglecart. His mossy foot pressed down on the bottom part. With a single tug, he ripped the whole top free, sending screws flying in every direction.

"Well, that's going to save us some time," Wily said with a smile. "Rip the top off another two."

With the gearfolk dispatched and the rust fairies still trapped in their cages, everyone focused their attention on helping Wily build his giant mechanical bird.

"Those are going to be the wings," Wily said, pointing to the snagglecart bases.

"They're made out of metal," Pryvyd said. "Don't you think they'll be too heavy to fly?"

"Says the man with a floating arm of bronze," Wily said.

"I didn't think you were planning on using magic," Pryvyd countered.

"Science is just a different kind of magic," Wily said. "You attach the wings while I build another chop-o-lot."

The group worked fast, but before long, the motorized drawbridge descended and two dozen of the Infernal King's mechanical soldiers exited the fortress.

"You keep building," Lumina said, cracking her knuckles. "I'll handle the gearfolk with Impish and Gremlin."

Wily nodded and turned his attention back to the flying machine. Pryvyd and Righteous were working in perfect unison. Pryvyd held the two pieces of metal in place while Righteous, holding the screwdriver, spun swiftly. Odette smiled at Wily as she twisted herself into a tight spot that only someone as flexible as her could reach. Wily had always thought building by himself was fun, but it was much more enjoyable working together.

"There are the intruders," one of the incoming gearfolk screamed as she rolled toward them with a spiked trip stick.

The two-dozen gearfolk rattled toward them in a swarm of rolling metal.

CLANG. CHUG. BANG.

A speeding snagglecart with Lumina standing on top of it came blasting toward the gearfolk with its mouth open. The mechanical soldiers tried to scatter, but five of them couldn't move fast enough and were swallowed up by the wheeled prison cart.

"Nice driving," Lumina called out from the top of the snagglecart to Gremlin, who sat inside in the small seat normally reserved for a rust fairy.

Gremlin spun the steering wheel and the snagglecart made a wide turn as it came back to scoop up another cluster of gearfolk. Inside the belly of the cart, the gearfolk were screaming and banging their metal fists against the rib cage.

"More problems," Odette said as she looked off to the hills in the west.

Wily didn't even want to look. He followed her eye-line to see the scorpions from Carrion Tomb skittering toward the fortress. Stalag sat on the largest, with his black robes flapping in the wind.

"I'll hold them off as best I can," Pryvyd said, then turned to Righteous. "Are you with me?"

Righteous hovered before him, rubbing his thumb against his fingers as if in thought.

"I take that back," Pryvyd said sincerely. "You've always been on the right side. I've been in the wrong. The real question is 'Will you let me join you?'"

Righteous saluted and pulled the sword from Pryvyd's sheath.

"I'm ready to be a knight again," Pryvyd said with a noble air that Wily had never seen in him before. "Thanks for never doubting me."

Pryvyd grabbed his spiked shield from his back. Together, he and Righteous marched off to face the scorpions and the oglodytes that were mounted atop them.

As Stalag approached, he held his arms up—but not to cast a spell. He was holding them aloft in apparent surrender.

"I have a proposition for Wily," Stalag called out with his most friendly and calming voice (which was neither). "Come back to the tomb with me. I'll admit I wasn't always the best father to you. But I never abandoned you like your birth parents."

"You lied to me my whole life!" Wily shouted back. "And now you're just afraid my father will kill you if he finds out that I've escaped."

Stalag's blood-cracked lips turned into a grimace.

"You're not fooled as easily as you once were," Stalag said, growing angry. "We can do this the other way, too." He gestured to the oglodytes flanking him. "Get him."

The oglodytes leaped off their scorpions and started swinging their axes.

Pryvyd and Righteous met them in combat. Four oglodytes attacked Pryvyd from both sides as Righteous kept the stinging scorpions at bay.

Stalag fired off crackling black arrows of energy at Wily, Roveeka, and Odette, who were still furiously constructing. Moshul lifted a large piece of scrap metal and used it to block the incoming bolts.

"Attach the chop-o-lot to the front of the bird," Wily said to Odette and Roveeka. "Make sure the gears line up to the cogs on the base."

Wily hurried around the mechanical bird, tightening screws, as he dodged Stalag's magical arrows. Pryvyd and his floating arm wouldn't be able to hold off the cavern mage for much longer. In fact, Sceely and Agorop were already charging for Wily.

Wily eyed the metal contraption that he had hastily built with his friends. It had two wings with adjustable flaps, a rotating tail, and a rudder to control the steering mechanics. A crank-powered chop-o-lot was attached to its front. There were no seats or harnesses. It wasn't elegant, but it would have to do.

"It's finished," Wily called out to Lumina, who jumped off the speeding snagglecart, "or at least as close as it's going to get."

Roveeka gave a sharp kick to Agorop, sending the oglodyte tumbling backward, then turned and ran to Wily's side. She extended her hand and offered Wily one of her two precious knives.

"Take Pops with you," Roveeka said.

"It's okay," Wily said.

"No, I want you to take him," Roveeka said. "You

may need my pops to defeat yours. Besides, I've got Mum here to keep me safe."

Wily took the curved knife and tucked it into his waistband.

"Thanks," Wily said as he bounded up to the rudder of the mechanical bird.

Lumina climbed aboard as well and took a seat on the frame beside the rudder.

"Hold on," Wily said. "I'm not sure how fast this is going to go."

Lumina tightened her fingers around the metal beam beneath her as Wily began to twist the crank. The chop-o-lot at the front of the bird began to spin. A strong current of air blew across Wily's cheeks. He cranked harder.

The bird began to move.

Very slowly.

Not nearly fast enough to lift off the ground. This wasn't going to work.

"It doesn't have enough power to take off on its own," Wily said as the chop-o-lot spun and spun.

The metal bird dragged across the ground.

"You tried, Wily," Lumina said, "but it's not going to work."

"Just like you," Wily said with determination, "I don't give up."

Wily called out, "Moshul, I want you to pick up the bird and throw it as far as you can."

"Are you crazy?" Odette said from the ground. "It's not like tossing a knife."

"Once it's in the air, I think it will stay afloat," Wily said, "at least for a short while."

Wily turned back to Moshul.

"We're only going to get one shot at this, so give me your best toss."

Lumina hopped off the mechanical bird.

"What are you doing?" Wily said to his mother.

"You don't need any extra weight," she replied. "You'll have go up there without me. Take my bag and remember: the Sun Stone will be in the room just beyond the throne room. Destroy it and the fortress will lose its power. All the traps will stop working and we'll be able to come and help."

Wily grabbed the bag and swung it over his shoulder.

"I believe in you," Lumina called back as she squeezed her fist. "You're stronger than even you know."

Wily hoped his mother wasn't putting too much faith in him. But if she believed, he would, too.

"Okay," Wily called back to the moss golem. "Now."

Moshul lifted up the bird in his mighty arms and tossed it. Wily could feel the machine lift at first and then start to dip. He was not ten feet off the ground and he was already heading back down. Wily cranked the chop-o-lot as fast as it would go. It felt as if his arm might actually snap right off.

The bird was only a few feet off the ground. He prepared for impact.

Then the machine began to level out. Wily cranked even faster. He had to get it higher into the air.

"Whash you thinking your doin'?" Sceely yelled as her scorpion galloped alongside the mechanical bird.

With a running jump off the scorpion's tail, Sceely landed on the wing of the mechanical bird. The flying machine lurched to one side.

Wily kept cranking as he pulled back on the rudder. Out of the corner of his eye, he could see Sceely heading for him with her venom-tipped trident.

"Put thish metal flying thingy down before we both get all killy," she said.

Sceely didn't wait for a response. She lunged at Wily with her weapon. He rolled from his seat just in time.

Wily was now standing on the left wing, trying to maintain his balance as the machine wobbled in the breeze. Sceely came after him again. He pulled out Pops to defend himself.

"We were friends for all those years in the tomb," Wily pleaded. "And you hated Stalag. You were terrified of him."

"He told me he won't go all hand-choppy on me if I najeflume you."

Najeflume was the oglodyte ambush term for "capture and drag home with wrists tied and mouth stuffed with soiled pantaloons."

Sceely swung her trident and Wily ducked out of the way. At that moment, he realized they were about to crash into the outer wall of the Infernal Fortress.

Wily dove for the rudder and pushed it hard to the right. The wing flaps adjusted accordingly. The mechanical bird banked hard.

Sceely lost her footing and rolled backward along the body of the machine. She was now dangling from the end.

"Hold on," Wily called out.

As he turned back to save her, her webbed fingers lost their grip. She went tumbling downward. Wily heard a splash below as she hit the moat and sunk into the water.

Wily darted back to the rudder and yanked it again. The bird soared upward.

He aimed the nose of the mechanical bird for the balcony of the fortress's high tower.

The bird was soaring for the open balcony window fast.

Very fast.

Too fast.

21

THE THRONE OF A KING

There was nothing he could do but hold on tightly. Slowing down was not an option. Wily was going to crash. He gripped the rudder and braced for impact.

The beak of the flying machine hit the stone balcony railing, shattering it. The bird did not slow down, though. The head of the construct went straight through the open balcony door. The wings were far too wide to fit and snapped off in a howl of twisting metal.

Wily's arms trembled as the bottom of the metal flying machine ground against the marble floor of the fortress's high tower, sending a shower of sparks flying. The tail of the machine slid back and forth, striking the elegant couches and side tables that furnished the grand hall. The machine came to a sudden stop when the nose struck an alcove wall adorned with a large tapestry. The hanging carpet was torn from its brackets and came tumbling down onto Wily.

Beneath the heavy cloth and silk, Wily took a moment to breathe and take stock of himself. Nothing seemed broken. He was alive. And he was in the Infernal Fortress. Now he just needed to find the Sun Stone that powered the Fortress and destroy it.

Wily reached up and pulled the tapestry off his head.

He was in a royal hall. There was enough seating for at least a hundred guests. On every wall was either a painting or a tapestry that depicted a grand moment in the history of Panthasos. Before the Infernal King, this must have been a place for large celebrations. Besides the destruction his mechanical bird had caused, everything was immaculate. Wily knew how difficult it was to keep the smallest area free of dust and grime, let alone a space as big as this.

He stepped off the flying machine and adjusted his tool belt and the satchel, which his mother had handed him before takeoff. She had told him to get to the throne room. He began moving silently and swiftly farther down the hall, deeper into the fortress.

Wily stopped before a portrait of the royal family: a mother, a father, and three children, two boys and a girl. *Were they my grandparents? And is that little boy my father as a child?*

Then he heard the squeak of metal armor. It sounded close. Wily ducked down behind a sofa, pressing his cheek up against the velvet armrest.

He held his breath and peeked out as a gearfolk passed by, pushing a wet mop along the marble floor. He stayed perfectly still until the metal automaton passed.

Wily stood up and was surprised to find himself face-to-face with a man only a few inches taller than himself. The man had wisps of gray hair that streaked through his otherwise short brown locks. His cheeks had a shiny pink glow as if they had been cooked gently in a steam oven. And though he was hardly muscular, the man's fingers were tough and calloused like Wily's.

"The gearmaids won't be pleased when they see the mess you've made in the Hall of Portraits," the man said, adjusting the glasses that rested on his nose. "I'm not pleased either."

Wily slowly reached for Pops, which was tucked into his back pocket.

"How dare you skip past all my traps?" the man said, arching his eyebrow. "You're a cheat."

At once, Wily was certain who this man was. He puffed his chest and stepped forward. Wily had been thinking about this moment for the last week. Every step toward the Infernal Fortress had been building to this.

"Hello, Father," Wily said, his gaze steely.

Kestrel Gromanov looked as if many disparate gears had suddenly interlocked in his mind, forming a perfectly functioning conclusion.

"I was wondering why Stalag was out of the tomb," Kestrel said. "He let you escape. A foolish mistake on his part."

"That's the greeting you have for a son you haven't seen since he was a baby?" Wily asked.

Why do I care what this man says at all? He is a monster.

"I've been receiving yearly reports on your progress," Kestrel said. "And I'm very pleased with the skills you've developed. I have even used many of your never-scapes here in the castle. They kill quite nicely."

That explained the Wake-No-More in the basement of the fortress. All of Wily's trap designs that Stalag had dismissed were not actually being rejected, but rather being sent in secret to the Infernal King for his own uses.

"Those were never meant to hurt anyone," Wily said.

"Yes, I know," Kestrel said. "It does seem that you

have quite the soft spot for people. Just like your mother. I'm sure you'll get over that in good time."

"I'm not like you," Wily insisted.

"I think perhaps you've misjudged me," Kestrel said. "Follow me."

Kestrel started to walk down the hall in the direction Wily had been heading.

"And don't even bother pretending you're going to use that dagger you have hidden behind your back," his father added. "We both know that violence is not something you're capable of."

Wily just stood there, unsure of what to do.

"Well, son," Kestrel said as he turned back, "do you want to see the throne that will one day belong to you?"

This was not how he'd imagined the raid proceeding. Yet the one thing he needed to do was get to the throne room. He followed after his father.

"I'm not sure why you and your friends think you could stop me," Kestrel said rather matter-of-factly as he walked on. "No one has ever been able to before."

"The Scarf has kept you on your toes," Wily snapped back.

"You mean your mother?" Kestrel replied.

Wily was caught off-guard. "You knew?" Wily said, almost to himself.

"Since the first time she blew up one of my snaggle-carts," Kestrel replied. "Who else would be as dedicated to ruining my life as her?"

"But if you knew . . . ?" Wily said.

"Why not just kill her?" Kestrel asked mildly. "I'm not the beast or monster you think I am. I just want order."

Father and son reached a room with three large chairs and a small stool opposite them.

"This is the throne room," Kestrel said.

Wily could see that beyond the chairs was an open door leading into a chamber filled with levers, winches, and gears, all operating under the glow of a Sun Stone.

As Wily came to a stop, he noticed the top of his satchel slowly open on its own. No, not on its own. Something, or rather someone, was inside.

Impish peeked her furry head out of the bag. She held a clawed finger up to her lips and whispered, "Shhhhh."

Kestrel paced in front of the three chairs.

"I am curious about what you've learned and how your brain operates," Kestrel said. "Here is the question that my father asked me when I was about your age: Which seat is the throne fit for a king?"

Wily looked at the three chairs.

"In fact, if you answer correctly," his father added, "I will spare you and your friends any harm."

Wily took a seat on the stool across from the chairs and looked at each one slowly. The first was made of bronze and had dragon claws on the armrests and feet. The second was ash black and floated a few inches above the ground. The third was made of polished wood inlayed with gold leaf and pearl.

Out of the corner of his eye, Wily watched as Impish snuck from his satchel and scampered silently away.

It was a riddle. He was excellent at riddles. But he knew he couldn't solve this one too fast. He needed to give Impish time to make her way to the machine room and snag the Sun Stone.

"Let me see," Wily said aloud. "The first chair is bold and strong. The person who sits atop it would rule like a dragon, fiercely defending his land and kin."

Kestrel nodded, clearly very interested in how his son thought.

"The second chair is laced with power," Wily said. "The person who sat on it would rule with magic from on high, looking down upon his subjects as slaves to serve him."

Kestrel waited patiently for the description of the third chair. Wily could no longer see Impish and hoped dearly that she had found her way into the hidden chamber on the other side of the throne room.

"The third chair is elegant and inspiring," Wily continued. "The person who took its seat would have the love and admiration of all, from sea to mountain."

"So which would it be?" Kestrel said, with a tinge of impatience. "Which is the throne of a king?"

Wily sat, thinking. He could tell his father wanted him to lose. Just to show how much wiser he was than his son. Wily could stall no longer.

"I know the answer," Wily said confidently. "The throne of a king . . . is the stool I'm sitting on. Simple and thoughtful. A true king considers every possible outcome before a decision is made."

Kestrel fumed.

"I wish you had just chosen the second chair like I did when asked the question," Kestrel said. "You could have joined me here, rather than being sent back to Carrion Tomb."

Kestrel slammed his fist against a secret pressure plate in the wall. From below Wily's stool, a snap cage sprung out from the floor, closing fast like two halves of a clamshell. But before they completely shut on Wily, the cage froze in place.

Kestrel looked confused, then turned to the antechamber. All the levers, gears, and mechanics had stopped moving.

"The Sun Stone!" Kestrel shouted.

Both Kestrel and Wily spotted—at the same time—Impish running with the Sun Stone sticking out of her tool belt.

Wily leaped from the half-closed cage and ran for his mother's ferret. Kestrel was quicker, though. He intercepted the small mammal and grabbed it by the tiny stub of what was left of her tail. He pulled the Sun Stone out of the tool belt and ran for a stone wall.

Where is he going? Is there a secret door there? His father reached the spot and with a quick flick of his wrist, opened a door to the maintenance passages of the fortress. He slipped inside.

Wily just barely made it to the door before it closed. He squeezed his body through as it shut behind him.

Ahead, Kestrel was running along the narrow passage. It was dark, save for the shafts of light shining through the secret spy holes that looked into the neighboring rooms.

Kestrel reached a precipice where a hanging cart was attached to an overhead cable. Jumping into the cart, Kestrel grabbed the hand crank connected to the cable's pulley system and began twisting it furiously.

Before Wily could get to the edge, the cart with

Kestrel inside started its way across the gap toward a platform on the other side.

Wily couldn't let his father get away with the Sun Stone. He looked around for some other way across the gap, but there was nothing else. No ledge or bridge. Wily looked over the edge. He could imagine the bone-crushing thud his body would make if he fell the ten-story drop.

Kestrel was nearly to the other side already.

Wily opened his trapsmith belt to look for some tool to help cross the gap. Screwdrivers, vials of lizard mucus, a bottle of slug slime sat in the leather pouch along with the gwarf's journal and the scroll tube his mother had given him with the map of where she searched for him.

Why couldn't there be a fully functional pulley cart in my pocket? That would be of help. Stay focused, Wily. Be creative.

Wily looked at the objects again. He had an idea.

He put all the objects back in his pouch except the map tube and journal. He popped the caps off both ends of the metal map tube, leaving it just an empty cylinder. Then he pulled out the leather drawstring that bound the journal and slipped it through the metal tube.

He backed up a dozen steps and then sprinted toward

the edge. Right before going over, he hooked his make-shift device over the cable and grabbed the leather strings in both his hands so that he was hanging from the tube.

The momentum sent him zipping out across the gap, the metal tube spinning rapidly along the cable above. It was a thrilling and terrifying ride. Nothing but his sweaty palms was keeping him from dropping to his death.

He made it all the way to the other side, where the hanging cart was dangling. Wily released his grip on the leather straps and tumbled onto the metal floor of the cart.

Looking up, Wily could see that his father was already halfway down a maintenance corridor that led to a machine room.

He sprinted toward him as the maintenance corridor suddenly sprung to life. The gears and levers began to move as if every trap in the fortress had activated.

Wily had to time every step perfectly to avoid losing his head to a swinging pendulum blade or his foot to the churning pistons of a leg crusher. The mechanics of the traps were suddenly as dangerous as the traps themselves.

At least, they would have been for anyone but Wily. His years in the tomb had taught him well. He wasn't relying on what he could see but on what he could hear and his knowledge of how machines operate.

CLUNK-GRR. It was the sound of a hammer setting a spinning blade into motion. Wily jumped, letting the ankle-snipper slice air beneath his feet. WHIT-TING. A dozen arrows had just been fired from a row of self-loading bows—which meant a dozen more arrows were going to take their place! Wily ducked as a mechanical arm swung overhead, holding twelve sharp-tipped projectiles.

Still, Wily made it to the other end of the corridor without even a small cut. He saw that the Sun Stone had been placed on a pedestal, which now glowed with energy. Nearby, he found his father putting on his infamous suit of armor.

"You might have had a chance of doing battle with me," Kestrel said just before lowering the helmet onto his head, "but you can't defeat the Infernal King."

Wily watched as the suit of armor whirred to life. Crackles of electricity danced between the fingers of the right gauntlet while the left transformed into an axe. Spinning blades rose and fell from the chest plate.

Wily reached down and touched Mum. *What can a knife do against the Infernal King?*

"Time for you to go back to your tomb, boy," Kestrel

said, his voice booming from the hole in the metal mask. "Or should I say hobgoblet? That's what Stalag made you think you were, right?"

"It doesn't matter if I'm a hobgoblet, elf, golem, or human," Wily said. "It's what's inside me that's important."

Wily dug his fist into his trapsmith pouch and pulled out a glass vial.

"Don't move," Wily said, holding the vial aloft threateningly, "or I'll stop you myself."

"Even the flames of the great lair beasts of old couldn't penetrate my armor," the Infernal King scoffed.

The Infernal King advanced with his crackling gauntlet outstretched.

Wily threw the glass vial at his father's feet. It shattered, sending green-speckled goo splattering on the ground and boots of his father's armor.

"A nice attempt," his father said, "but not as dramatic as you had hoped."

"I learned a lot about building traps in Carrion Tomb," Wily said. "But even more about keeping things tidy. First lesson for you: giant-slug slime is a sticky mess to clean up."

The Infernal King looked down to see that the slug slime had hardened quickly into a thick sap. Kestrel tried to lift his boot, but it was now held fast to the floor.

"Get it off!" shouted the Infernal King.

As Kestrel struggled to pull his foot free, Wily ran around him and snagged the Sun Stone from the pedestal. At once, the fortress went dead again. Every trap machine in the corridor turned off once more.

"I think it's time that *you* got a taste of being locked away," Wily said to his father.

22

A LAST RIDDLE

Wily often woke up in the middle of the night to the wail of the screeching stones cutting through the air. He'd grab for his trapsmith belt only to realize that it wasn't there. After a moment of panic, Wily would look around and remember that he no longer lived in the twisting corridors of Carrion Tomb. His new home was the royal palace of Panthasos. And there were no traps in the there. At least, not anymore.

Most evenings, he'd breathe a sigh of relief and roll over, quickly falling back to sleep. Tonight, though, he decided to walk the halls. He had been given a large collection of shoes, slippers, and sandals, but he preferred to go barefoot. The cool polished marble felt delightful on his feet.

Just down the hall, Wily stopped before a portrait that had been painted of his mother and father on their wedding day. Looking up at their smiling faces made him wonder if either could have ever guessed what twelve years would bring. He peeked into the neighboring room. It belonged to his mother; she had chosen the room that was closest to Wily. After all these years apart, she didn't like to be too far away. The curtains drawn around her bed signaled she was already asleep and couldn't scold him for tiptoeing out at this late hour.

Wily's father had a new home in the prisonaut, which had been converted from a place to confine the innocent to an actual prison for those who had done wrong. So far, there was only one resident.

Wily was hoping to add at least one more: Stalag. But the cavern mage was nowhere to be found. He and his oglodyte minions had fled while Wily's companions had raided the disabled fortress and helped Wily take Kestrel into custody. A week later, when Pryvyd sent the newly reformed Knights of the Golden Sun to Carrion Tomb to capture Stalag, the tomb and the mine below were nearly empty; only the giant slug and the Skull of Many Riddles had been left behind. (Both of which Wily had allowed to take up residence in the royal palace.) The knights searched Rivergate Woods and beyond for Stalag, but the cavern mage had covered his tracks carefully.

Wily continued down the hall to his favorite room in the palace: the library. There were shelves and shelves and shelves of books, so many that he couldn't count them all if he tried. Better yet, there were no explorers coming in and tossing them to the floor, looking for secret doors. They were just there for reading.

In the month since moving into the palace, Wily had spent many hours learning to read. He had made great strides, although he still found it to be quite challenging. The letters *b* and *d* looked an awful lot alike, and he often tried reading words from the back to the front, rather than the other way around. He was determined to learn even if it took him a little extra time.

He entered the library and was surprised to find Odette sitting there. She looked up from her book as he entered.

"Couldn't sleep?" she asked.

"I had the dream that I was back in the Carrion Tomb again," Wily said. "You?"

"Roveeka is a really loud snorer for such a small hobgoblet," Odette said. "It's like she has the nose of a cloud giant. I could hear her all the way down the hall."

Wily let out a laugh. Roveeka had made herself quite at home since the Infernal King's defeat. She loved having a room with a view of all of Panthasos and had even gotten used to sleeping on a mattress. Quite soundly, in fact. She would often doze until the sun was high in the sky, snuggling Mum and Pops in her arms like straw dolls.

"That's every hobgoblet," Wily said. "Back in the tomb, if I didn't shut the door of my sleeping chamber, it sounded like a hundred crab dragons roaring in unison."

Odette pulled over a stack of fairy tales.

"You want me to teach you how to sound out compound words?" Odette asked.

"Yes," Wily said. "But instead of the fairy tales, you can use *Wily Snare's Book of Inventions.*"

"Again?" Odette asked. "We read that one yesterday."

"And only got a few pages through it," Wily said. "It's very interesting."

Odette walked over and pulled the book Wily had taken from Squalor Keep off the shelf.

"While you find the page we left off at," Wily said, "I'll go get us cookies."

"The chocolate ones," Odette said, "and the cinnamon ones."

Wily hurried back out of the library and down the stairs. He passed through the sitting room, which looked out upon the garden. He often found himself staring out the windows here while he—

"What are you doing up?"

Wily spun around to see his mother sitting in an overstuffed chair. Across from her, Pryvyd reclined on a couch with his boots off.

"You're back," Wily said to Pryvyd. "Did you find Stalag?"

"We searched all the way to Cloudscrape, but still no sign of him. Or the oglodytes."

"Ahem." Lumina cleared her throat. "Don't think you can distract me. I asked why you were out of your room."

"I'm not tired," Wily said. "I was just going to do a little practice reading with Odette."

"She's up, too?" Lumina huffed.

"It's a bright moon," Pryvyd said. "Give them an hour or so."

Wily looked at his mom with pleading eyes.

"Okay," Lumina relented, "but Righteous will be checking up on you later."

"That's fine," Wily said, then quietly added, ". . . and I'm getting some cookies, too."

Wily hurried into the courtyard before his mom could respond. Once he was outside, he looked over his shoulder to glance back at them. For a second, he thought he saw Pryvyd holding his mom's hand. But he could have been wrong.

Wily passed by the giant slug that was sleeping by the lily pond. Moshul was there, too, holding Gremlin and Impish softly in his lap. Wily was about to call out to him, but before he could, Moshul put one of his large mossy fingers to the spot where his mouth would have been.

Instead, Wily practiced some of the new signs he had learned. *You're a good big brother.*

Moshul's jeweled eyes twinkled at the compliment. He gently rocked the two ferrets in his mushroom-covered arms.

Wily continued toward the stairs to the kitchen. He made it halfway across the courtyard when the Skull of Many Riddles flew into his path.

"Wily!" the skull said as it hovered in front of him. "A riddle for your life!"

"Really? Now? I'm just on my way to get a snack."

"It's a good one," the skull said weakly.

The cookies weren't going anywhere.

"Fine," Wily said.

The skull laughed with insane glee. A fiery green aura erupted around it.

"What has a mouth but does not eat?" the skull sang. *"It twists and turns but has no feet. It has teeth of stone—"*

"A cave," Wily answered.

The skull's flames disappeared. It looked rather disappointed.

"You got that one too fast," the skull pouted.

Wily continued through the courtyard toward the kitchen. The skull flew over to intercept him.

"One more?" the skull pleaded.

"One more," Wily said.

The skull, delighted, burst into glowing green flames again.

"What of yours now seems done," the skull sang aloud, *"but in fact has just begun?"*

Wily had to think about this one.

There were many things that had ended. His time in the tomb. His loneliness. His search for his family.

And there were many other things that had just begun. Like his new friendships, his sunny days in the palace, and his love of cookies. But he couldn't think of anything that was a perfect answer for the riddle.

"I give up," Wily said. "What seems done but in fact has just begun?"

The skull cackled victoriously and then gave the answer.

"Your adventure."

ADAM JAY EPSTEIN

spent his childhood in Great Neck, New York, when he wasn't aboard his father's sailboat. He spent many days sitting in the neighborhood park, traveling to fantasy lands in his head (occasionally when he was supposed to be doing his homework). In college, he circled the world on a ship and studied film at Wesleyan University. He is the coauthor of the internationally bestselling middle grade fantasy series The Familiars and the middle grade sci-fi series Starbounders. He has written film and television projects for Disney, Sony, Fox, MGM, Paramount, MTV, Hulu, Syfy, and Disney Channel. He currently lives in Los Angeles with his wife, two daughters, and their dog, Pixel.

ACKNOWLEDGMENTS

A BOOK BEGINS with inspiration, and mine started in elementary school. I want to thank my childhood friends Michael Kuo and David Garris, who helped instill in me a love of maps, elves, and magic. My parents for buying me countless Dungeons & Dragons manuals when I was still a reluctant reader of fiction. The masters of fantasy who sparked my imagination as a kid: J. R. R. Tolkien, Gary Gygax, Piers Anthony, Shigeru Miyamoto, Steven Spielberg, and Ray Harryhausen.

I need to thank my daughters Olive and Penny (with whom Wily and Odette share many traits) for being my first test audience and biggest fans. And to Mrs. Hulett's fourth grade class of '17 and Colfax Charter for allowing me to read *Snared* long before publication. Also many thanks to my village, which feels like a small town in a big city.

My gratitude goes out to my incomparable agent, Markus Hoffman. I cannot imagine a more thoughtful, persistent, and dedicated coconspirator in the literary world. Wily Snare would have never made it to the Above without you.

I want to thank the wonderful team at Imprint who has quickly made me feel at home. Nicole Otto, who during a particularly painful plane delay decided to pick up my manuscript to pass the time and has been a tireless advocate for it ever since. John Morgan, your insight and wisdom make me look smarter than I actually I am. Iacopo Bruno, I want to plaster my walls with the cover you have drawn (and, in fact, I have). Natalie C. Sousa, for turning this book into a work of art. Raymond Ernesto Colón and Alexei Esikoff, whose eyes for detail are unmatched. Erin Stein, editor in command, for taking me under your wing and allowing me to be part of the amazing family that you have built.

During the writing process, I wasn't alone. I had the constant companionship of Trader Joe's Chile Spiced Mangoes, Tejava Unsweetened Tea, Howard Shore's scores for *The Lord of the Rings*, and my blue, bubbling Lava Lite Lamp.

And the biggest thank you of all goes to my wife, Jane, for her love and patience. This book did not happen overnight, but in fact over many, many nights. And while I was just a few yards away, I missed you dearly during them. You are correct (as usual): the best is yet to come.

MORE DUNGEON-RAIDING ADVENTURE AWAITS!

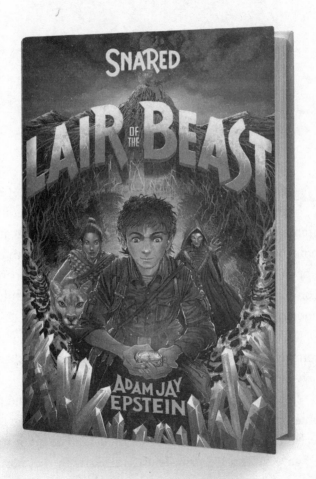

Keep reading for an excerpt.

1

MAZE OF THE DISSOLVED

At the end of a long torch-lit hall, four blinking eyes, each as big as a slither troll's fist, adorned a stone arch. They were restlessly shifting back and forth, scanning the area for intruders. Wily recognized the enchanted trap at once. There had been one just like it in Carrion Tomb, the dungeon in which he had spent his childhood.

"It's an Archway of Many Eyes," he explained to his companions, who were standing behind him in the shadowy entrance tunnel to the Maze of the Dissolved.

"I know what it is," Odette said, flicking a strand of blue hair from her face. "This isn't the first dungeon we've raided. More like the hundredth." The acrobatic elf gave Wily a big grin. It was still early in the morning, and she was always extra cheerful before lunch (even if they were deep inside a dangerous maze).

"Let's not exaggerate," Pryvyd, the one-armed Knight of the Golden Sun, said. "We've only explored eighty at the very most."

Righteous, Pryvyd's former arm, now disembodied and floating beside him, started moving its fingers as if counting in its head—not that Righteous actually had a head—or a body for that matter.

"Back me up here, Moshul," Odette said, turning to the giant moss golem.

Moshul, lacking a mouth, signed quickly to the knight with his big mud fingers.

"I'm not including the haunted temples or the swamp towers," Pryvyd countered.

Moshul signed back in response. Despite knowing Moshul for many months now, Wily was still struggling to learn sign language.

"That was a castle," Pryvyd said. "Not a dungeon."

Moshul signed again even more emphatically.

The knight relented. "Fine, if you include the temples *and* the towers *and* the castles, we might have raided a hundred."

Odette seemed very pleased with herself.

"I don't think the exact number of dungeons you've explored is important right now," Roveeka, Wily's adopted hobgoblet sister, interjected.

"She's right," Wily said. "Once those eyes spot us, an alarm will sound, and every creature in the maze will know we're here." He tapped his thumb against the wrist of his other hand. It was something he did when he was thinking hard, like when he was trying to solve a riddle or studying a complicated machine. Or coming up with a clever plan. "But that's only *if* the eyes spot us," he said with a sly grin.

He moved to Moshul's side and plucked a dark purple mushroom off his elbow. The moss golem was like a walking garden: vines, toadstools, and vegetables shared space on his lush green body with a hundred different kinds of crawling worms and insects. Wily handed the plump fungus to Roveeka.

"Roveeka," Wily asked, "how's your aim with mushrooms?"

"Almost as good as it is with knives," Roveeka said, weighing the mushroom in her hand.

During Roveeka's days in Carrion Tomb, she had served as a knife tosser, helping to ambush adventurers searching for treasure. Although she still carried her two precious knives, Mum and Pops, she had been practicing throwing other objects as well since escaping the dungeon with Wily.

"It needs to land just below the arch," Wily said. He turned to the others. "When it strikes the ground, move fast. Don't worry about being quiet. It's an Archway of Many Eyes, not ears."

Pryvyd and Righteous gave Wily matching bronze-plated thumbs-ups.

"Fast is not a problem for me," Odette said with a

grin. "The question is whether I'm going to do backflips as I sprint."

Roveeka cocked her hand and, with a flick of her lumpy wrist, flung the mushroom through the air. It hit the stone ground just below the archway and exploded into a cloud of thick black smoke.

"Now!" Wily urged the others.

Odette shot forward in a dazzling sequence of leaps and tumbles, quickly disappearing into the smoke ahead. Moshul grabbed Roveeka by the back of her shirt and tucked her under his arm as he took heavy lumbering steps toward the archway. With Righteous floating by his side, Pryvyd charged ahead, his bronze armor squeaking, clearly in need of a greasing.

Wily raced after his companions into the cloud of black. He could hear his companions moving on either side of him, but the smoke was so thick that he couldn't even see his own fingers. Worse still, with each breath, his nostrils were invaded by the pungent odor of rotting carrots. The purple mushroom had created an excellent smoke screen, but its smell left much to be desired.

After three dozen steps, Wily emerged from the smoke. With a loud gasp, he sucked in a lungful of cave air. His vision cleared, and he saw Odette already standing there, twiddling her fingers as if she had been waiting hours for his arrival.

Pryvyd, Moshul, and Roveeka stepped out of the haze just as it began to dissipate.

"Did the eyes spot us?" Pryvyd asked, "or did we get by unnoticed?"

"There's no way to tell out here," Wily answered. "The alarm doesn't sound in the main tunnels of the dungeon, only in the hidden maintenance tunnels. We'll just have to go deeper to find out."

The group continued down the long corridor to a room whose walls and ceiling were covered in snaking roots and dangling vines. In the middle of the room, a stout man with a tool belt stood on a ladder. He was busy sharpening a row of swinging blades and seemed completely unaware of their presence.

Wily knew at once that this man had to be the maze's trapsmith. Just a few months ago, before he learned that he was in fact the Prince of Panthasos, Wily had been just like him, stuck doing the mundane tasks that kept the dungeon operating smoothly. He had spent years sweeping Carrion Tomb's crypts, sharpening the spikes, feeding the rats, and greasing the gears of the crushing walls.

As the stout man performed his monotonous task, he sang an off-key tune:

"Got to keep the blades swinging, swinging, swinging overhead.

Got to keep the snakes biting, biting, make sure they're well fed.

Got to keep the slime dripping, dripping, then I'll go to bed."

Wily hadn't sung while he performed his duties, but now, thinking back, perhaps it would have made the endless stretches of dullness pass more quickly. Of course there was a lot Wily didn't know back then. He had been convinced by Stalag, the master of Carrion Tomb, and his surrogate father, that he was a hobgoblet rather than the human he actually was. And he had believed Stalag's other lies as well: that the sun would melt the skin clean off his bones the moment he left Carrion Tomb. And, worst of all, that his parents had been killed when in fact they were very much alive. His mother was the famous freedom fighter known as the Scarf and his father was the recently dethroned Infernal King. There were still mornings when Wily woke from slumber and didn't think any of it was true—just a wild, dizzying dream.

Wily spied the exit on the other side of the room. He signaled his friends to move for it. The trapsmith did not seem to have the slightest clue that Wily and his fellow adventurers were silently sneaking through the shadows along the perimeter of the room. As Wily and the others tiptoed out of the room of dangling roots, he heard the trapsmith begin a new song.

"My sister kissed a troll down by the river.
She thought that kiss would break a cursed spell.
But that troll was just a troll down by the river.
Still, she married him and now they're doing well."

The group moved down a short hall and stopped before the entrance to a cavernous room strewn with skulls and bones. Peering inside, Wily could see a giant fanged bear sleeping soundly on the floor. A spine of sharp needles grew all the way down its back.

"A quill grizzler," Pryvyd said with a tremble of fear.

Although Wily had never seen one in the flesh before, he had heard stories of this fearsome creature. It was rumored to be capable of tearing a dragon in two with a single twist of its mighty fists. But, at this moment, it was extremely difficult to imagine this particular quill grizzler doing anything of the sort; it was snuggling a fluffy stuffed sheep while sucking on its own clawed thumb.

"Ohhh," Roveeka said, "he's so cute."

"Adorable," Odette added. "When he's not ripping your arms off."

"Shhh," Pryvyd said, "I'd rather not wake him."

Wily and his fellow adventurers walked silently through the cavern. As he moved past the snoring animal, Wily thought about how just yesterday he had been enjoying a plate of cookies in the palace garden with his mother, thinking his days of dungeon crawling might just be over. Then adventure had called on him once more.

Since the defeat of the Infernal King, Pryvyd and the Knights of the Golden Sun had been desperately searching Panthasos for Stalag. If the rumors were true, the pale-skinned master of Carrion Tomb had been crisscrossing the land, meeting cavern mages, dungeon lords, and catacomb witches with a promise: if they joined his army and helped him overthrow the new prince—Wily—no longer would they have to hide away in their caverns, dungeons, and catacombs behind traps and foul beasts. They could keep their treasures in the grand castles of the Above. They could live in the sunlight without the fear of being driven away and having their loot stolen.

Despite Pryvyd's best efforts, Stalag always managed to stay ahead of them. Wily's mother had offered a reward to anyone who knew where Stalag would head next, but no one had come forward with anything helpful.

Then, yesterday, an old locksage smelling of dried squid had visited the palace with a valuable piece of information. The locksage told Wily and his mother that while he didn't know where Stalag was, he knew of something that could help them find him. He said that the Sludge Duke kept an enchanted compass hidden inside his Maze of the Dissolved. Unlike a normal compass, which always points north, this enchanted compass could point in the direction of anything that the holder wished to find as long as they had a small bit of metal to give the compass the magnetic scent, whether it be an incredible treasure, their true love, or the cruel surrogate father who had kept them trapped in a dungeon for the first twelve years of their life. The Sludge Duke had created the compass to find his lost Ring of Rodents, the only thing that made him happy, but when the compass led him to a bottomless pit, the furious duke buried it deep within the maze, promising misery for all who hoped to retrieve it.

The locksage said that getting to the compass would be very tricky and dangerous; it would take some very talented dungeon explorers to survive the maze. Fortunately, Wily and his companions were just that.

With the quill grizzler still nursing his clawed thumb, the group hurried out of the large room and down the next hall. Wily kept his eyes down, scanning the floor for pressure plates and traps. He was startled when a gruff voice called out from up ahead.

"What are you doing here?"

Wily looked up to see a boarcus leaning against the wall, holding a plate of salted crab. The hairy, tusk-faced guard stood tall with surprise.

"How'd you sneak past the Archway of Many Eyes without sounding the alarm?" the boarcus asked, the words slobbering through his large flabby lips.

"We didn't sneak past," Wily bluffed, while out of the corner of his eye, he could see Roveeka reach for Mum and Pops, tucked into her waistband. "That would be impossible. We're the new recruits."

There was a reason that boarcus were never used as the first or second or even third line of defense. They were extremely dim and thickskulled. Their primary purpose in a dungeon was to wander about and look intimidating.

"Hmmm," the boarcus said, thinking hard. "Then shouldn't you be in the Hall of Swords?"

"Yes," Wily said, feigning embarrassment. "We must have gotten lost. It is a maze, after all."

The boarcus considered this last statement for a long moment, then came to a conclusion. "That makes sense," he said, relaxing his overworked brain.

Roveeka let her hands fall from her knives.

"Here's my trick to keep from getting lost," the boarcus added with a curl of his snout. "You never walk around without a map. I got the Sludge Duke to draw one on the back of my shield. That's what I did."

The boarcus pulled the shield off his hairy arm and proudly showed them the inside. Etched into the metal was a very detailed map of the Maze of the Dissolved.

"What a brilliant idea," Odette said. "Maybe I can borrow yours."

"Hmmm," the boarcus considered. "If invaders come, I may need my shield to defend myself."

"As if any invader would get past the quill grizzler," Odette said with grin.

"You do have a point," the boarcus said. "But I don't know . . ."

"What if I offered to trade you my leftovers at dinner for it?"

With that, the boarcus handed the shield over to Odette with a smile big enough to lift his tusks.

"So where are we?" Pryvyd inquired, gesturing to the shield map.

"You really are confused," the boarcus said. "We're right here." He pointed to a spot near one of the shield's handles.

"And just to get my bearings," Wily asked, "where is the enchanted compass?"

"The treasure room is here." The boarcus moved his finger to a spot at the bottom of the shield, then pointed down the hall before them. "Which is that way. But you want to be heading in the other direction, back past the quill grizzler."

"And what did you draw down here?" Odette asked, pointing to a dot in the center of the shield map.

"I can't tell what you are pointing to," the boarcus said, squinting through the tufts of hair just below his eyes. He leaned in for a closer look.

As he put his tiny eyes up to the etched map, Odette smashed him in the face with the back of the shield. The boarcus collapsed to the floor.

"He'll just take a quick nap," Odette said with a glint of mischievousness in her eyes.

Wily and his companions took off fast, following the map on the back of the shield toward the treasure room. Moshul scooped Roveeka up and tucked her under his arm to make sure she didn't slow them down; Roveeka might have been an expert knife- and mushroom-thrower, but she wasn't a sprinter, and there was no time to waste. It would be only a matter of time before another guard found the unconscious boarcus lying on the floor and raised the alarm to alert everyone that there were intruders in the maze.

Despite the danger of traps and monsters, Wily was surprised to find he was overcome with a feeling of joy and freedom. Yes, life in the palace was wonderful, with its courtyards and banquets and grand libraries, but along with all the good came a tremendous amount of pressure. One day, not long from now, Wily would officially take the throne and become King of Panthasos. He would be responsible for the safety and well-being of everyone in the land. That would be an overwhelming task for even the most brilliant grown-up, let alone him, someone who only just last week had learned how to peel an orange. (One didn't find a lot of citrus fruits in a dungeon.) There was still so much that he needed to learn, including how to read, which was proving to be more of a challenge than he had expected. Wily didn't want to disappoint everybody. At times, the pressure to live up to expectations was suffocating him.

But here in a dungeon, in a world he knew like the back of his hand, with his friends by his side, all the worries of the Above seemed very far away.

THE WAKE-NO-MORE